NO SUCH THING
as the
REAL WORLD

An Na

M. T. Anderson

K. L. Going

Beth Kephart

Chris Lynch

Jacqueline Woodson

WITH AN INTRODUCTION BY
JILL SANTOPOLO

NO SUCH THING
as the
REAL WORLD

Stories about
growing up
and
getting a life

LAURA GERINGER BOOKS

HARPER TEEN

An Imprint of HarperCollinsPublishers

HarperTeen is an imprint of HarperCollins Publishers.
No Such Thing as the Real World
Copyright © 2009 by HarperCollins Publishers
"Complication" copyright © 2009 by An Na
"The Projection: A Two-Part Invention" copyright © 2009 by M. T. Anderson
"Survival" copyright © 2009 by K. L. Going
"The Longest Distance" copyright © 2009 by Beth Kephart
"Arrangements" copyright © 2009 by Chris Lynch
"The Company" copyright © 2009 by Jacqueline Woodson

Library of Congress Cataloging-in-Publication Data
No such thing as the real world / M. T. Anderson . . . [et al.] ; with an introduction
by Jill Santopolo. — 1st ed.
   p. cm.
 "Laura Geringer books."
 Summary: Six award-winning young adult authors present short stories featuring
teens who have to face the "real world" for the first time.
 ISBN 978-0-06-147058-5 (trade bdg.)
 ISBN 978-0-06-147059-2 (lib. bdg.)
 1. Short stories, American. 2. Young adult fiction. [1. Interpersonal relations—
Fiction. 2. Coming of age—Fiction. 3. Short stories.]
PZ5 .N526 2009   2008022583
[Fic]—dc22   CIP
                                             AC

Typography by Amy Toth
09 10 11 12 13   CG/RRDB   10 9 8 7 6 5 4 3 2 1
❖
First Edition

Dear Reader,

*W*hen Laura Geringer and I started putting this collection together, we talked a lot about the "real world." We talked about the line that separates the time when you're a child, when most things are provided for you, from the time when you're out on your own, taking care of yourself and forging your own way. That line is often not an age but an event: Sometimes it's graduation, sometimes it's a moment of self-discovery or a time of great loss. And sometimes—as with the characters in many of these stories—we're thrown into this so-called real world before we're ready.

In the John Mayer song that inspired the title of this collection, there's a line that says, "I'd like to think the best of me/ Is still hiding/ Up my sleeve." I think that line probably applies to all the characters in the stories here. From high school graduates to teenage moms to dancers to pawn shop owners, all these characters are thrown into the "real world," discover it's not exactly what they imagined it would be, and struggle to find themselves.

If you are between the ages of fourteen and nineteen, and if you have ever struggled with the "no such thing" aspect of the "real world," we invite you to submit your own short story for possible publication in the paperback edition of this collection. We're looking for stories with strong characters and strong plots that show us where you think that dotted line between childhood and adulthood truly lies and the ways in which the real world can be different from what you expected. You can find more information about this contest in the contest section of our website: www.harperteen.com.

But before you write, be sure to read the spectacular tales that An Na, M.T. Anderson, K. L. Going, Beth Kephart, Chris Lynch, and Jacqueline Woodson have contributed to this fine collection.

Jill Santopolo
Senior Editor

Contents

Complication

An Na

The flickering streetlamp outside the window casts a tangerine glow in the small bedroom. The unsteady light pushes past the venetian blinds, throws trembling horizontal stripes on the empty beige walls. The shadows stretch up to the ceiling, where, taped over the bed, there is a slightly skewed poster of paradise: blinding white sand, flat stretch of blue-green crystal water, and the lone couple walking far in the distance. The vision circumscribes each day like bookends.

In the corner, near an open door that leads to a dark hallway, a small makeup mirror sits squarely in the middle of a desk. Pencils and pens pushed aside. A chemistry textbook balances precariously on the corner. The pages of a returned English short story marked with heavy underlinings and bold exclamation points litter the floor. Amid all the clutter, Fay leans forward and bows her head to the mirror as if readying for prayer. Without blinking, without a single tremor in her hand, she draws the black eyeliner along the moist pink edge of her lower lid.

A phone rings in the distance. An older woman holding a baby against her hip walks into the hallway and turns on the light. She sets the baby on the floor and answers the phone. The baby is drawn to the light of the mirror, crawling quickly down the hall. Fay's eyes flicker toward the movement. She reaches out with her foot. And kicks shut the door.

2

Fay is bumped from behind as two women push past her on their way up the stairs to the bouncer guarding the door of the club. The taller blonde takes each step as though she is on stage. Her hands running through her hair, hips rocking, long black fur coat open with each step to reveal the length of her bare legs.

The bouncer takes one look at the women and barely shakes his head. The taller one steps forward, lightly places her finger at the knot of the bouncer's tie. She shrugs and lets her coat fall off one shoulder, revealing the tight corset top pushing up the creamy half-moons of her breasts. He gives her a quick, embarrassed smile but refuses to move.

A strangled scream breaks the night. The woman wheels around and glares down at the crowd watching her performance. And in the harsh overhead floodlight, all the years of her life crawl out of the shadows and ravage her face.

Fay draws her jean jacket closer to her body as the two blond women pass her and walk across the street. Fay scans the street once more before shoving her hands deep into her pockets. Andy is late as usual; Fay's eyes follow the sound of laughter to the market, where the women are flirting with the elderly Asian man putting away the flowers for the night. Some people stamp their feet and warm their hands with their breath. The first bitter night of winter catches an unlucky few without the proper clothing, and they complain loudly to each other about how this place isn't worth the wait, but still they remain standing. Crashing music punctuates the night every time the door opens and lets in the next chosen group. Time passes and the crowd outside begins to dwindle.

A blade of panic cuts into Fay's body and she begins to think of running away. From this place. From him. From everything. Inside her pockets, her hands ball into fists and she pushes them against her ribs, focusing on the crush of flesh against bone. Stay, she tells herself. Stay and wait. She can't lose it now. Not now. Not after all this time. All the planning. Fay scans the street once more, and before she can think, her feet are carrying her across the pavement.

"Fay!"

Andy comes striding across the street, her long hair loose and wild, the dark curls framing her electric-blue eyes, open wide with excitement.

Fay stops and shouts in relief. "What the hell, Andy! I've been standing out here for over an hour."

"I'm sorry, I'm sorry. The F train was a mess." Andy studies Fay's face carefully. "Damn, girl. You lookin' good. You wearing that blouse I lent you?"

Fay turns away for a second and then nods.

Andy pulls on the hem of Fay's jacket. "Come on, let's get inside before my toes fucking freeze and fall off."

Andy quickly makes her way up the steps and greets the bouncer with a glancing kiss to the cheek.

"It's hot tonight, Andy. Watch yourself." He grins and opens the door. The music slams into their bodies and swallows them whole as they step into the darkened club. Fay and Andy immediately peel off their outer layer and hand them over to the girl at the coat check. Fay stares out at the crowd and self-consciously adjusts the thin straps of her silky black blouse. The undulating bodies, hard breathing, and alcohol fumes saturate the air, coating her skin with the moisture, the music, the warmth. It soaks into her tense, frozen body and floods her senses. Fay closes her eyes against the dizziness and takes a deep breath, trying to control the uncontrollable trembling rising up from the soles of her feet.

"Come on," Andy says, and takes her hand. They push past the crowd standing at the bar and make their way to the back hall.

A few couples linger along the darkened narrow space. Andy stops at a closed door and turns to meet

Fay's eyes. She leans in close. "Are you sure you want to do this?"

Fay nods.

Andy pulls back with a reluctant shrug and knocks loudly.

A tall man in a dark suit cracks open the door, his face deep in shadow. A narrow band of red light shines out from the room that he guards, and Fay strains forward to peek inside. The man notices Fay's interest and the door begins to close, but when Andy steps forward, he pauses. Andy begins to whisper.

Fay gazes into the room. The low red lighting makes it difficult to see, but Fay glimpses the plush sofa where a few older men recline, their legs crossed, their arms splayed out along the length of the backrest. And then her view is blocked. By a woman. Her body is lean and long, and as young as Fay's.

Andy steps aside and the man opens the door just enough to allow Fay to enter. She steps through. The door shuts behind her.

3

The foyer echoes with the sound of their entrance, the black marble floors amplifying the sigh of coats being removed and the crush of gravel under Fay's heels as she takes a tentative step forward. He drops his keys on a dark wooden side table next to a minimal arrangement of orchids and long, dark, twisting branches. He turns his head to look back at her, and the soft light from the sconce on the wall catches his eyes. Fay's throat closes in recognition. His eyes are green. Just like his brother's. The red lighting in the club had fooled her into thinking that they were blue. But she should have known. The same shade as a newly unfurled leaf.

"Do you want some water?" he calls back as he quickly steps into the darkened space. The city lights beckon from all around the room, the floor-to-ceiling windows clear as air. Fay stares out at the view, and for a moment she is filled with the desire to walk straight ahead, off the edge, into the waiting night. A light in the kitchen flicks on, and Fay's gaze is broken.

"Are you hungry?" he asks, and she can hear the

refrigerator opening.

Fay walks forward and enters the kitchen. Every surface gleams with the shine of meticulous cleaning. Fay walks to the large center island and leans her hip against the edge of the black marble countertop.

"I can make you toast," he offers with an embarrassed smile, and holds up the bag of sliced white bread.

Fay shakes her head.

He puts the bread back in the refrigerator and then walks over to the island to stand across from her. The silence between them opens up wide and dark as the stone that separates their bodies. He stares across at her, and she can see his thoughts surfacing and breaking the still pool of his face. His chagrin. His desire. His fear. Slowly, she lifts her hand to her neck. Her fingers trail along the line of her collarbone until she feels the silk strap of her blouse barely hanging on to the rounded cliff of her shoulder. A push. The strap falls. Cool air on warm skin. Her nipple contracting in response. Her body stiffens when he slowly closes his eyes.

With an abrupt turn he stammers, "You know what, I'm starved. I could use some toast right now. What do you say? Toast with a little butter? I think I have some strawberry preserves, too. Yeah, let me check." He flings open the refrigerator. "Sorry, I lied. It's not strawberry. It's raspberry. Do you like raspberries?" He says all this without turning back to her. The skin at the base of Fay's throat flushes red, naked with emotion. She quickly pulls up the strap.

"Just some butter," she says. "Please."

He nods and pulls the bread out of the refrigerator.

✱

They stand next to each other silently chewing their toast. He has smeared his slice with raspberry jam. They chew thoughtfully, glancing at each other once in a while. He wipes his mouth with the back of his hand.

"Wish I had more food in the house, but I've been traveling a lot lately."

Fay nods and longs for a napkin but for some reason feels uncomfortable asking.

When he finishes with his toast, he turns and begins to study her face. Fay holds her breath and lets his eyes wander over her forehead, her cheeks, her lips, her eyes. Fay believes, now, he will come to her. Now, she has him.

His eyes move away, and he begins to study the piece of toast in her hands. "I know how to cook," he says.

It takes a second for the statement to sink in and then she explodes, bits of bread flying from her mouth. She clamps her hand over the laughter. Her stomach aches from the effort of trying to restrain herself.

He is pained at her disbelief. "No, really. I do know how to cook."

"Yeah, right," she says. "Like what? Toast?"

He grins down at her. "I'm serious. I can make you whatever you want."

"You have no food."

"I haven't gone shopping."

"Check out this kitchen. It looks like it's never been touched, but you want me to believe that you know how to cook."

He glances around. "Melinda does a good job cleaning, especially when I haven't been around for a while."

Fay chews thoughtfully and wonders if she should ask where he has been.

"How old are you?" he asks, just as she pops the last bit of toast into her mouth. She exaggerates chewing and flashes her fingers in response.

He nods as though he already knew. "Are you still in school?"

"Just graduated," she says.

"What are you going to do next?"

She glares at him. "What's with all the questions? Are you like some wannabe guidance counselor or something?" She shakes her head and stares at her fingers shiny with butter and crumbs.

"Sorry," he says, and pulls open a drawer. "I didn't mean to pry."

He hands her a white cloth napkin.

"Then don't."

"I just want to get to know you."

"So you won't feel guilty when you fuck me?"

He moves away from her and paces, his hands locking together behind his neck. Finally, he turns and says, "I don't normally go to those places. I run a nonprofit. I go to jazz concerts. I like watching movies at home," he says.

Fay looks up from wiping her hands. "And you think those men you were sitting with in the club aren't just like you? Look. The less I know about you and the less you know about me, the better it is."

"Fay, I've been looking for you."

Fay stares at him evenly. "Do you know how many times men like you have used that line?"

"What do you mean, men like me?"

"Men who are looking for someone like me. Someone young enough to be let into that room I found you in."

He shakes his head. "No, no. It wasn't like that."

Fay steps closer and stands in front of him. "Then what was it like? What is it like now?" Fay places her finger on the top button of his dress shirt.

He holds absolutely still. Fay begins to unbutton the shirt. He catches her hand and slowly lowers it to her side. "I just want to talk. I really do. Talk to me."

She meets his eyes. "What the hell are we supposed to talk about?"

He releases her hand. "My brother."

Fay exhales. The length of her spine suddenly prickles with heat. She turns her back to him and stares out the windows, letting the darkness of the night seep into her body. "What do you want to know?"

"Why was he so unhappy?"

"He wasn't always like that," Fay says, and she begins with the first time that she met him.

He caught her outside the club that first night, having a smoke with Andy. He had passed them only to double back to ask them for a cigarette. There had been something about his eyes when Andy showed him the crumpled pack. Those crazy beautiful green eyes dropping in disappointment as a simple smile of regret lifted one corner of his lips. Fay couldn't help but offer him a drag off hers, and as he stood there talking to them, she felt him drinking her up until she felt empty with need.

It is only when the room begins to lighten with the red orange colors of dawn, making Fay yawn suddenly, that he realizes the time. He looks out the windows taking in the sunrise.

"Your mom isn't waiting up for you?" he asks quietly.

Fay shakes her head.

"I should take you home," he says, his eyes unable to meet hers.

"I can sleep here."

He nods. "I should take you home."

✱

Fay opens the door to her apartment and notices the silence. They have gone out. The weariness comes on immediately, as soon as she steps inside and closes the door, as though the curtains are closing after a long performance. She hangs her jacket on the hook and shuffles to her bedroom. Her eyes droop with the anticipation of bed, with the knowledge that sleep will finally return to her as fast as it has been running away from her for the last few days. Sleep. She lies down and stares up at her poster of paradise. The dream comes and carries her away.

Even with her eyes closed, she knows her mother is in the room. Fay pretends she is still sleeping, but her mother can hear the difference in her breathing.

"What happened?" her mother asks.

"Nothing," Fay replies without opening her eyes.

"Nothing?"

"Yes."

"You met him?"

"Yes," Fay says, and pauses, unsure of whether to reveal that he had known about her. Had, in fact, been looking for her. But this piece of information doesn't change anything. Her plan remains the same.

"Luke's taking a nap," her mother says.

Fay can hear her walking to the door.

"Are you going to see him again?"

"Yes." Fay opens her eyes and gazes up at the ceiling. The color of the water fills her senses, her mind, deepens the longing in her chest. "Yes. Tomorrow."

4

He never touches her. Sometimes she can see his hands trembling, but he never reaches for her. He holds them together or puts them to use. He cooks for her. Makes her breakfast after they return from the club. Toast and eggs. Sometimes huevos rancheros with warm corn tortillas that he presses out by hand. She sits on the counter and watches him work, his forehead notched in concentration. And then there are the moments when he just stares. As she is lifting the napkin to her lips or setting down her glass of orange juice, she feels his gaze.

Unexpectedly. The verdant green of his eyes darkening with intensity until they are the color of old jade, and that is when she must focus on her feet. Placing them squarely on the surface of the floor. Feeling the solid ground beneath her. But he keeps his distance. Continues to ask her questions about who his brother had become in the years that they had lost touch. Two brothers in the same city, but never speaking. Fay wonders why they fell out with each other but waits to see if it will be revealed before she needs to ask.

In the club he is protective. Shielding her from other men's eyes. He blocks their view, and when she dances for him, he sits nearby, immediately standing up as soon as the song is over. She feels him watching her when she moves, feels his eyes traveling along the length of her body, and that is when she is sure of him. And yet, when she has had enough of the music and he brings her back to the darkness of his loft, he simply watches her eat and asks questions.

"How is it?"

She nods and spoons more of the oatmeal into her mouth. A ring of maple syrup lines the bowl.

"Of all the things that I can cook, you wanted oatmeal tonight." He sighs.

She smiles as she stirs some of the syrup into the beige goop. "I like oatmeal," she says. "It's comfort food."

He leans forward suddenly and touches her arm. Fay jolts back, jerking her elbows off the table.

He reaches his hand out to her, beckoning her to come forward. "Sorry, I didn't mean to startle you. I just saw that mark."

Fay glances down at the light-brown oval birthmark near her elbow. When she was a small child, her father used to kiss that same spot and whisper that it had been given to her at birth by the lips of an angel. Fay had always believed him, feeling inwardly blessed and lucky until the day when her father didn't return home. And then she knew he had lied to her, just as he had lied to her mother.

When he continues to wait, his arm stretched along the length of the black marble, the blue veins beneath his pale skin exposed and mapped, she reluctantly places her hand in his. He turns her arm slightly to get a better look and then rubs the spot with his fingers as though he might clean it off like a coffee stain. She turns her head away at the gentle pressure of his hand holding hers. The slight scrape of his calluses as he touches the birthmark. How can his touch feel so different from someone who grew up with the same mother. The same father. In the same house. How can they be brothers, she wonders?

"It's like someone kissed you right there and left a smudge," he says.

Fay nods. "My father used to tell me it was a kiss from an angel."

He smiles. "Yes. Exactly."

"I used to believe everything my father told me," Fay says.

"I did, too."

"But then I found out that he lied." She glances down at the mark. "The day my father left, all his angels fell to earth and became specks of dirt."

"You don't believe in angels?"

"No," Fay says, and turns away so that he can't see the lie in her eyes. "Tell me something: Why did you stop talking to your brother?"

He studies the mark a moment longer before he carefully releases her hand, slowly pulling away as a lover might gently ease himself out of bed so as not to wake the other. She longs to grasp his fingers, to pull his hand back, but a shyness steals over her. A shyness that turns to terror at the realization. She cannot feel this way. Fay stands up quickly. She should have grabbed his hand when she had the chance. Grabbed it and pulled it to her.

He studies his palms. "I took my brother to Thailand with me when I had to oversee the water treatment plant that was being built with the funds from my nonprofit." He pauses and stands up. Begins to pace. Fay sits quietly waiting. He turns away and says, "He raped a young girl in the village, and we had to run before the authorities could catch up to us. When we got safely back to the city, I never spoke to him again."

An emptiness. A void. The words enter into Fay's body, and the edges of her memory dissolve, flooding her thoughts until all she can see is the ghostly image of herself that night as she lay beneath him on the stairs in his apartment. She had wanted to be with him that night, she reminds herself.

Fay stands up. "I need some water."

"Let me—"

"I got it." She quickly walks over to the cabinet and pulls out a glass. She knows where everything is now. She knows the refrigerator will have neatly lined up bottles of fresh spring water and mineral water and wine and beer.

Fay pours herself some mineral water, savoring the tiny bubbles. She concentrates on the fizzy sensation. He carefully approaches her as though she is standing on a tightrope. A balancing act of sheer will. He stops a few feet away. Fay waits to see if he will ask the inevitable question.

"I have to leave in a few days," he says. "It'll only be for a few weeks, I promise." He leans forward and rests his forehead on his forearm.

The sun pushes over the edge of a neighboring building and pours in through the wall of windows. Fay stares at his hair, at the shy undertones of browns and reds scattered among the black and gray. A cacophony of midnight autumn colors that dance only under spotlight.

"You'll probably eat pizza every night," he says, more to himself than to her.

Shallow sips of air, her chest rising and falling in rhythm to the swirling dust caught in a beam of light. She stares at a painting on the far wall while he talks about where he will be going, what project he must oversee before he can return.

"I can see you once more before I leave," he says. "Can you make it Friday?"

She nods.

She can feel him studying her face. This need to constantly know what she is thinking has become familiar to her. She turns and smiles brightly. Too brightly perhaps.

"Hey, don't worry. I'll still be here when you get back. It's not like I got a million other things to do while you're away," Fay says.

He begins to protest, launching into his speech about how she could be whatever she wanted to be if she put her mind to it. Her mind turns inward, but her eyes remain alert so he won't know the difference. She has a call to make.

5

Fay sits on the bottom step of the stoop, her hand protectively spotting Luke as he pulls himself upright using the upper step as his prop. He has been trying to walk, and already there is a large knot by his ear where he hit the corner of the coffee table before he went flailing to the floor. He pats the step and smiles up at Fay. She smiles down in return.

"Girl, what is that child doing touching that nasty sidewalk?" Andy yells from nearly the end of block as she strides toward them.

"It's not the sidewalk, Andy," Fay yells back. "It's called the stoop."

Andy is upon them in a leap. She sweeps up Luke and kisses him loudly on the neck before returning him stunned and confused back to the steps.

Fay scoots over, and Andy sits down next to her.

"Where your mom at?" Andy asks.

"She went down to the grocery store."

Luke begins to crawl over Fay's lap, headed over to Andy, his eyes focused on the bright round buttons of her coat.

"Don't let that child slobber on my clothes, Fay," Andy says, her voice deepening for a second to her usual bass.

Fay grabs Luke and glances over at Andy, noting the dark circles under her eyes.

"You look like shit," Fay says.

Andy sighs and leans back against the steps. "Thanks, girl. Just what I needed to hear. Damn hormones are messing up my sleep."

"You up your dosage?" Fay asks.

Andy nods and opens her eyes. Her blue-tinted contact lenses swim in a pool of tears. "Why do they have to make being a woman so goddamn hard?"

Fay reaches out and brushes the loose tendrils off Andy's forehead. "It's a hard club to join. That's why you have to be fierce."

Andy straightens up and takes a deep breath. "That I am, love. That I am."

Fay turns her eyes back to Luke, who has managed to traverse all the way over to the railing and is grinning so hard, he begins to drool. Fay smiles. "I wish I could take a magic potion and be a girl again."

"Me too, baby."

"I never got that. Those years to be just free and happy. All I can remember is working. Either lugging around some stranger's kid or helping my mom when she was trying to get that catering business going."

"Oh yeah, I remember when your mom was doing that."

Fay hits Andy's arm. "You do not. We didn't even know each other then."

"Yes we did. I moved downstairs from you when we were eight and your moms was flipping out because you had accidentally poured too much cornstarch into the pudding she was making for that wedding or something. I can still hear that slap."

Fay's knuckles brush her cheek. "Yeah, that was a bad day."

Andy hugs her from behind. "Come on. All those years made you a hard-ass. And without you pushing me all the time to be myself, where would I be?"

"You mean, if I hadn't beaten up every kid who made fun of you, where would you be?"

"See, that's what I'm talking about. Damn, hard-ass. Yeah, where would I be if you hadn't been my body-guard?"

Fay leans back into Andy's arms and smiles at the memory of the two of them walking the streets like they were some tough shit. They had been so young. If only they could have stayed girls for a moment, a lifetime, longer.

"What's happening with you and the man?" Andy asks.

"Nothing," Fay says, and quickly reaches out to grab Luke before he can use the railing to make his way up the steps. Luke arches his back and cries when Fay lifts him up.

"What do you mean, nothing?" Andy yells over the crying.

Fay stands and rocks Luke to sooth him. "He just wants to talk all the time. And cook for me."

Andy flings up her hands in laughter. "First time inside and you manage to land a hausfrau."

"He's no housewife, and if you would come inside with me, you could see for yourself," Fay says, setting Luke back down on the steps.

"You know my night in the Roxanne room is on Sundays. All them preachers ready to unwind after shouting the gospel all day."

Fay keeps her eyes on Luke and says quietly, "I need something, Andy."

Andy runs her large hand down the length of her wig. "What you got in mind?"

"Something to knock him out."

"That's easy enough."

"Nothing crazy, Andy," Fay says.

Luke lets go of the step, his chubby legs locking into place, and he stands there, looking up at Fay with wonder.

Fay whispers quickly, "Look, Andy, he's standing."

Andy turns just as Luke loses his balance and falls on his butt. Andy clicks her tongue. "Yeah, baby, get used to it. That's what life is all about."

Fay picks him up and kisses him gently on the forehead. She whispers so that only he can hear. "Don't worry. I'll be here."

6

They leave the club earlier than usual. Fay leans against him and lifts her chin to the door. He immediately gathers their coats. He doesn't disguise his annoyance at the club scene, but he goes because she likes to dance. They walk out the side entrance into an unusually warm winter night. The snow pushed to the edge of the sidewalk has begun to melt and pool into the cracks and dips of the uneven pavement. Fay stops at a particularly large puddle, pondering how best to navigate around it in her open-toed black heels. He has walked into the street to see if he can spot any cabs in the distance. When he turns back to signal that there is one coming, he sees her dilemma. He steps quickly over to her side.

"I think I can hop over," Fay says.

Without a word, he sweeps her up in his arms, and as he gallantly steps over the water, he loses his footing, almost dropping her before he rights himself and lets her down on the pavement with a grunt. The gesture is sudden. Unexpected. Ridiculous. Fay begins to laugh. She tries to steady herself on her heels.

"That was not smooth," she says, looking up at him.

"You're heavier than you look," he responds.

She makes a muscle and points down at her biceps.

"All muscle, baby. I could destroy you." She doesn't tell him how she got to be so strong. How carrying Luke up four flights of stairs to the apartment, especially now that he is getting to be a toddler, creates muscles that never existed before.

He takes her hand and leads her to the street, his other hand flagging down the cab coming toward them. The cab stops, and as he opens the door for her, he whispers, "I'm already destroyed."

She silently slides into the cab.

Fay waits the entire night before she has the opportunity to drop the tablet into his tea.

"Why do you like that green tea so much?" she asks as he is fixing her a sesame bagel and whitefish. He starts to decorate her plate with cucumbers and tomatoes. He calls it garnishing, but she knows it's a way for him to get vegetables on her plate.

Gently, he slices the tomato. "It's an oolong tea, and I like the buttery aroma of it. And the flavor is rich but clean."

"Can I try some?"

He looks up at her in surprise. "Really?"

She shrugs. "Sure, why not? Does it have caffeine in it?"

He raises one shoulder. "A little. Not like coffee, though."

She picks up the delicate miniature cup and pretends to take a sip. When he turns to pull the bagel out of the toaster, she slips in the tablet and places her palm over the mouth of the cup, grabbing the entire thing and giving it a quick shake. The tea burns her skin, but she focuses on melting the tablet quickly. She sets the cup back on the counter and checks to make sure everything has dissolved.

"How was it?" he asks as he turns back around and places the bagel on the plate.

"It was good," she says.

He glances at her before picking up the cucumber to finish with the garnish. "Did you take a second to smell the aroma?"

She shrugs. "Sure. Butter. A hint of nutmeg." She grins.

"It's not a cookie," he says, and slices perfect, almost translucent, green circles of cucumber.

She focuses on eating her sesame bagel quickly, but in her peripheral vision she watches him sipping his tea. She wonders how long it will be before he begins to feel the effects. Andy said it was a tranquilizer, but what did that mean? Will he fall asleep right here in the kitchen? Will he start to get sleepy and move to the sofa or the bedroom?

"You're going to choke if you keep eating that fast," he says.

"I'm starving," she says with her mouth full.

He gestures toward the tomatoes and cucumber. "Come on, at least try a little bit with the bagel. It won't kill you to eat something healthy."

Fay grabs the entire neatly lined row of cucumbers on her plate and shoves it into her mouth.

He begins to laugh. "That wasn't quite what I meant, but I suppose it'll do the trick."

Fay watches him stifle a yawn.

"When are you leaving?" she asks.

"Tomorrow afternoon."

"Should I go and let you sleep?"

He shakes his head and starts to protest, but

another yawn overwhelms him. "Sorry, I'm just feeling exhausted all of a sudden." He pushes away from the island and blinks quickly. "I wanted to burn you some of my music so that you could listen to some good stuff for once. Maybe when I get back, we could go to some other clubs."

She nods. He has talked about going to jazz clubs. Maybe catching a concert. She listens while staring at the empty teacup in his hands, his fingers absent-mindedly caressing the smooth porcelain. She thinks about the drug coursing through his body. This is the only way. The only way. The sudden hum of the refrigerator makes her aware that the room is silent. Fay lifts her eyes.

He is staring. She waits to see if he will suddenly pull away or turn his back. Do something, anything to break the tension and keep her at a distance. Or will he yield? She steps toward him. A band of panic narrows his eyes. "I should burn you those CDs," he says quietly, but he remains standing in place.

She takes another step.

The teacup in his hands begins to tremble.

She takes another step and reaches out to take the cup from him. He slowly releases his grip. She sets the cup on the counter, her eyes never leaving his. Slowly, she rises up on her tiptoes and leans forward, her forehead brushing against his lips. She moves her face slowly, as though she is dancing for him at the club. Her temple. Her eyes. She can feel his lips parting, the gentle push of his tongue as he tastes her skin. Her heart contracts for a second when he lifts her up and she realizes that her feet are no longer on the ground. She is floating. Floating. She closes her eyes and raises her lips. And she knows that from this point on, every kiss will taste incomplete without the lingering salt of tears.

In the bed he refuses to let her undress, only wants to hold her. He strokes her hair, and she can smell the toasted sesame of her bagel clinging to his shirt mixed with the evergreen scent of soap on his skin. His fingers press into her scalp as though he can feel her thoughts, and he begins to mumble about why she needs to go home. And then, slowly, she feels his body relaxing. His arm twitches. She waits a few minutes longer and then carefully she moves.

She takes off only his shirt and covers his pants with the sheet. She strips completely and positions herself almost on top of him without covering his face. She reaches over and turns on the lamp. With her camera phone extended as far as her arm will allow, she begins to take pictures. One after another, moving and angling her body for better shots. Finally, when she has enough photos, she gets up. He flings an arm across the pillow. She turns off the light and dresses quickly.

In the hallway leading back to the living room, she stops in front of a photo of the two brothers when they were teenagers. Her age. Possibly younger. She studies their faces. The similarities in their cheekbones and eyes. Their lips are pronouncedly different. One is full while the other is thin. She stares at their faces until, suddenly, she runs for the bathroom. She throws up everything.

7

From four flights down she can hear Luke crying. By the time she reaches the door, his cries have become choking wails.

Fay walks in, and her mother holds out Luke.

"He's had a temperature all night and he won't drink anything."

Fay takes him into her arms. "But we're almost done weaning. I don't know if I have any more milk."

Her mother walks away. "Your body knows."

Fay sits down on the couch and unbuttons her blouse, putting him to her breast. Immediately he begins to nurse, but when her milk will not come, he pulls back in frustration and howls. She rocks him, but he only wails louder, his body tense with pain. She sits down again and focuses on making him well. A mother will provide for her child. She puts him back to her breast, and his time when he begins to nurse, she can feel her milk letting down. He finally quiets and gazes up at her peacefully. Fay looks into his eyes. Green as a new blade of grass. Just like his father.

8

The letter has been composed for months. The first and last part of her plan. Ever since she discovered, after his death, that he had a brother. A younger brother who lived in the same city. A brother starting to haunt the same places. The same club. The same room. Only this time she would not be caught outside unawares. Naïve. This time she would be the one in control.

"You send the letter?" her mother asks, walking into Fay's room.

"Not yet." Fay keeps her eyes on the poster. Luke sleeps quietly curled along the side of her ribs.

"What are you waiting on?"

"He won't be home for another week."

"Then it'll be sitting in his mailbox when he gets back."

Her mother turns around to leave but lingers for a second longer in the doorway as though she has something else to add. As though she is the one directing the plan. And maybe she is. Fay understands how much her mother has had to sacrifice since Luke was born. Since Fay decided to keep the child against her mother's warning. And what could her mother really say? She had been even younger than Fay when she got pregnant. But unlike her mother, Fay knows what she wants. Has known from the moment Luke was born. They must leave. This apartment. This life. Return to the home her father left so many years ago. The birthplace of her father, her grandfather, her great-grandfather. An island she has never seen except in pictures, as a vacation place for the wealthy. A paradise. A dream. To Fay, the island harbors a childhood of memories that seem more real to her than her own. Even if he lied about everything else in their lives, she holds on to her father's descriptions and stories of his island like a religion, a leap of faith. She needs to believe he told the truth when he said he had a boyhood of simple pleasures. And more than anything in the world, she wants to be able to give that childhood to her son.

The request is simple. She knows he has the funds. His brother did as well, but he died before Luke was born. Before she even realized that she was pregnant. She's not asking for the world. Only what is fair. For her and for Luke. Just enough to start over. She can go to school at night. And yet, for some reason, she can't seem to mail the letter with the photos. After everything, she can't slip the slim white envelope into the mailbox.

Her mother taps her fingers against the doorjamb. "You didn't tell him about Luke, did you?"

"No," Fay says. "Luke is mine."

Her mother nods and then leaves the room.

Fay hears Luke's lips smacking in his sleep as though he is still nursing. Her breasts feel raw and tender, but Luke's fever has finally broken and he sleeps peacefully. A mother will provide for her child. Fay reaches over and picks up the envelope.

9

Three weeks later Fay checks the post office box she has set up specifically for the plan and finds a small green envelope. Inside, there is no letter. No note. Only a check folded in half. Fay pulls out the small square and checks the envelope again. It's stupid, but for some reason she thought he would write. She quickly buries her disappointment, but an ember lingers in her chest, burning fast and hard before it is stamped out completely. She unfolds the check. It is double what she requested. The sheer audacity of the zeros lined up like cans in a shooting gallery infuriates her. She slams shut the small metal door of the post office box and checks the amount again. It's a joke. He's mocking her.

There's no way the check will clear. He is refusing to cooperate. Fay has prepared herself for the inevitability of the situation. A picture will be mailed to his work-place. Nothing too risqué, but interesting enough that his office might begin to talk. There will be another letter. This time with the threat of police involvement. Sex with a minor. It would be his word against hers, and with the photos and witnesses at the club, it won't be too hard to make her case. Fay walks out onto the street and crumples the check, burying it deep in her pocket. Tomorrow. She will mail the picture and letter tomorrow.

Her mind is still on the money when she rounds the corner and begins to walk toward her apartment. Her eyes focused on the sidewalk, her body braced against the freezing wind. She goes over the plan again and again, thinks about all his possible reactions. She has prepared herself. She is ready. And that is when she spots him. Sitting on the stoop, his dark wool coat draped on the steps. She pauses midstep.

He sees her and stands up quickly, waiting to see what she will do. Fay bows her head and continues walking. She hurries past him, refusing to acknowledge his presence. Takes the steps two at a time and fumbles in her coat pocket for her keys.

"Did you get the check?" he asks.

She pulls out the key and slides it into the front lock.

"It's real," he says. "You can cash it right now if you want."

She turns the key and leans her hip on the door.

"Or we could just keep going."

She takes a step inside and then turns around to shut the door behind her.

"Please listen to me," he says. "Fay. I want to be in your life."

Fay's anger pushes her forward. "Shut up. Just pay me what I'm owed. I don't want a boyfriend. You think I'm an idiot? You think just because I let you take advantage of me that I'm just some stupid thing that you can play with?"

He walks forward, but Fay threatens to close the door and he stops.

"No, I don't think you're stupid. In fact, just the

opposite. I didn't know what to expect when I started looking for you. My brother left behind so few clues. But now that I've found you, I don't want to lose you."

Fay shakes her head. "You're rich. You travel all over the world. People respect you. And I'm supposed to believe that you want to be with me? How does that make sense?"

"Why does it have to make sense? Why can't it be that I feel connected to you? Maybe it's because of my brother, or maybe it's that I like talking to you or the way your eyes just kill me. I can't explain it except to say that I feel it and I know you feel it, too, Fay."

A wind blows the dust and trash across the streets. Fay wonders about angels.

"Be with me, Fay."

Can they return to the heavens after falling? Can they still fly even with scars?

"Do it for Luke."

She grips the edge of the door and keeps her eyes on the street. He knows. How could he know? She watches a man pushing an empty grocery cart up the sidewalk. The wheels rattle and the metallic clatter accompanies his whistling. How could he not know? The question is: How could she have been so naïve? He has all the resources in the world. He could take away everything.

"You really should have asked for more," he says, and takes a step forward.

She steps back.

"You can cash that check and do whatever you want, but if you stay with me, Luke will always have more."

Fay waves to the man passing by and then says, "What are you going to give him that I haven't already? Who the fuck do you think you are?"

"His uncle."

Fay rushes to close the door. She doesn't care about the money, the plans. She needs to hold Luke right now. Hold him and never let go.

He jams his foot in the door. "Fay, please. I didn't say anything sooner because I didn't want to scare you off. I wanted you to trust me. I want to be in your lives. I can give him anything he wants. You know that. He can grow up secure and happy."

"Money doesn't buy you any of that," Fay yells, and

kicks his foot out of the way. "Haven't you wealthy idiots paid someone to help you figure that out yet?"

He holds up his hands. "I understand. But money does help you do other things. It gives you options. Isn't that why you asked me for the money? So you and Luke would have options?"

"Fuck you. He owed me that money. He owed me for everything he did." Fay brushes aside the tears of anger welling up. Goddamn it. She hates when her heart betrays her this way. "You owe me," she states.

"Be with me and I'll take care of you. I'll take care of you and Luke. I'm trying to do the right thing." He steps backward and holds out his hands. "Let me love you. Let me love Luke. I'm not a bad man, Fay. You know that. I'm not like my brother. He was a lot of things that I couldn't understand. Let me try and fix some of his mistakes."

Fay looks out across the street. Stares at the gray-and-brown buildings lined up like tired old men waiting for a wind to blow them all over. She has lived on this block all her life. Watched men and women hustle for a living. Watched men and women die before living. She may be young, but she has lived long enough to know, shackles come in many forms.

"I'll be good to you. I'll cook for you. I want to know you and Luke. That's all."

Fay stares at him. The shade of a nearby building cuts a diagonal line across his face. The green of his eyes in shadow, dark as a forest, old as money. This is a complication she has not anticipated. What would she be giving up for all that he is offering? What would she have to take? It's never free. But a part of her wants to believe him.

She remembers the feel of his arms that last night together. The feeling of floating. The taste of salt on her lips. She could imagine him being a kind father to Luke. A kind man. And maybe he could love her. Maybe she could love him. If she believed in happily ever after. In angels. He watches her for a sign, his need to know exactly what she is thinking. She lifts her face, raw as the winter wind, and lets him read her as she slowly closes the door. She was never for sale.

10

The warm water laps at Luke's feet. He toddles in the sand, the uneven surface an obstacle course for his balance. Fay catches him up and throws him high into the sky. She had always dreamed of the colors. Blues and greens and summer white draped with rainbows. But she hadn't been prepared for the textures and sounds. Slippery scratching sand next to slippery silk water. The scorch of sun on a bare back. The rhythmic, soothing sound of the waves breaking along the shore. Before, she could not have imagined such a world existed even if she had tried. Now, she can't imagine having ever been away. She runs with Luke across the sand. She runs and slips and slides and falls and gets up and runs again like she's never had the chance to do before. The image of the poster jumps into her thoughts as they run back toward the water. Far in the distance, Fay believes, she can see the angels soaring up to the rainbows. Shaking the dust and dirt from their wings. They stretch for the heavens. Flying far and fast, scars and all.

An Na was born in Korea and grew up in San Diego, California. She is a graduate of Amherst College and received her MFA in writing children's literature from Vermont College. An Na's first novel, *A Step from Heaven*, won the Michael L. Printz Award and was a National Book Award finalist. She is also the author of *Wait for Me*, an ALA Best Book for Young Adults, and *The Fold*.

The Projection:
A Two-Part Invention

M. T. Anderson

 *A living room in a lakeside cottage. There is a fieldstone fireplace, an old sofa, and a comfortable chair with an ottoman. There are some knickknacks: figurines and a few low-grade trophies. Indistinct photos hang on the walls. There are some appliances of mysterious purpose here and there. They are made up of spheres and piping, cowling, a few horns.*

Sam sits on the chair. She looks expectantly at Alec. Alec appears to be waiting. They are apparently seniors at some boarding school. They look seventeen or eighteen, ready to graduate.

Sam looks artistic—lots of ringlets, which she must have worked on carefully. Throughout the opening of the scene, she has the look of someone who knows secrets, someone who is delighted—if shy.

Alec does not appear to be shy in the least. He is generally at ease with himself. He knows he is handsome. Nonetheless, their entry into this scene is awkward, if amiable. For a long time, there is silence. They do not know how to act around each other. Finally, Alec speaks.

ALEC: Man and wife.
SAM: Yeah.

They don't know what to say. Alec wanders around the room, bending down to peer at things. Sam waits, still delighted. She watches him, on occasion. She seems a little nervous.

ALEC: Man and wife.
SAM: Whom the Lord hath joined, let no man put asunder.
ALEC (*after a pause—cutely*): Nice place we've got here. . . . Nice.
SAM: The summer place.
ALEC: Yeah. Where the summer happens. Darling.
SAM (*smiling*): Darling.

ALEC: And the winter.

SAM: I love the winters.

ALEC: We have great fires. When it's cold outside.

SAM: When the snow's on the windowpanes.

ALEC: Here we are, honey.

SAM: Should we light a fire?

ALEC: It's the middle of the summer.

SAM: The kids collected kindling.

ALEC: We'd swelter. The smoke wouldn't rise.

SAM: You need to fix the flue before the weather gets colder.

ALEC: Is that the kind of thing we talk about?

SAM: Sure. Or I could fix the flue.

ALEC: You're good with your hands. You're handy.

SAM (*increasingly sly and playful*): The workbench is mine. All the tools. You never come down there. You're afraid you'll find me welding.

ALEC: Yeah. I call it "the Outback." You disappear for days. I hear the circular saw. You get that look in your eyes. There's something that needs to be built. So I say, "I guess you'll be going to the Outback now, honey."

SAM: Sure. I'm a gal who knows how to put flanges on stuff.

ALEC: What are flanges?

SAM: Exactly. Stay away from my workbench, bastard.

ALEC: The Outback.

SAM: Keep your distance. You're one giant thumb waiting to get whacked.

Alec ranges around the room, looking at things.

SAM: You sure you don't want a fire?

ALEC: You're all the light I need, honey.

SAM: Darling.

ALEC: Sweetie.

Alec keeps inspecting the walls.

SAM: The McMasters aren't up yet. It looks like no one has driven down their drive since the thaw.

ALEC: They never come up until the middle of July. They always spend the Fourth in D.C.

SAM: I wonder if their daughter's still a painted whore.

ALEC (*laughs*): Now, hey there.

SAM: Please. I wouldn't let that child near our dog, let alone our son.

ALEC: Son? Jesus.

SAM: She just renamed herself something. Their daughter. (*Snapping her fingertips, trying to remember.*)

ALEC: Nikki-Lu. With two K's and no O.

SAM: See? She's ready for a strip joint.

ALEC: Kids these days . . . Sluts and trollops, all of them . . . I don't know what the McMasters did to deserve the daughter. They're solid. They entertain well. That was a great bonfire last fall.

SAM: It was lovely.

ALEC: I like to see you drunk. You laugh a lot. What the fuck are all these machines?

SAM: Appliances.

ALEC: What kind of appliances?

SAM: I don't know. It's the future.

ALEC: I mean, what are they supposed to do?

SAM: Beats me. Turn one on.

ALEC: No fucking way. What do they do?

SAM: How the hell should I know?

ALEC: You're the one who's good with a band saw.

SAM: You're the one who's good with a credit card. You bought them all.

ALEC: I'm good with a credit card?

SAM: Whatever.

ALEC: I can't picture that.

SAM: I can. You get a boyish glint in your eye. It's completely charming. You hum the *William Tell* overture. Next thing, *bam*. We have some new . . . I don't know . . . gamma-ray toaster oven or electron swiveler.

ALEC: I don't even know the *William Tell* overture.

SAM: Budda-bump, budda-bump, budda-bump, bump, bump.

ALEC: Oh. Do you bitch me out when I buy a new gadget?

SAM: No. I look at you like you're an idiot, but a lovable idiot. We take it out of its box and try to figure out how to put it together. We sit in the middle of all the packing material for about an hour after, laughing hilariously, going, "Where the hell is sprocket G?"

ALEC: I buy them, you set them up.

SAM: I'm good with my hands.

ALEC: Yeah. And I can't stand to read instructions.

SAM: It's a little pathological.

ALEC (*protesting—a routine*): There aren't any people in the diagrams. It creeps me out. Everything moves by itself in those fucking pictures. The screws all suck up into their holes. And the plug is there crawling toward the wall. All the parts are looking at each other like they're getting cozy. Dotted lines. The whole thing comes together without anyone touching it. Like the world is empty except for machines.

SAM: It's rough, honey.

ALEC: I can't stand it. And when there are people in the pictures, they don't have faces. Maybe just a nose. They're completely blank and white. They put shit together, and that's it. There's a . . . I don't know . . . a . . .

SAM: Sterility?

ALEC: Yeah. Like they can install, but they can't care. They don't give a shit.

SAM: They can't enjoy their own appliances.

ALEC: Those instruction books freak me the fuck out. I

can't even touch them anymore. They're like some post-human Book of Revelations.

SAM: That was good.

ALEC: Thank you, thank you.

At this point, they are smiling at each other. They are each delighted by the cleverness of the other and their banter.

SAM (*suddenly shy again*): We're good at this.

ALEC (*not shy at all*): We are. (*Lies down on the sofa. He taps his feet together.*) Brett and Farooq have to case the joint. They have to be thieves.

ALEC: I think it's supposed to be Brett's joint. And he doesn't know his joint is being cased.

ALEC: Really?

SAM: That's what Daley said.

ALEC: Sucks for Farooq. He's like the least criminal person I ever met. A bunch of us were in Framingham the other day, and he found out he was going to be back like fifteen minutes late for prefect duty and he fucking freaked on us and forced us to get a cab. It cost like forty bucks to get back. It was rush hour. It was insane.

SAM: So thievery will be good for him. He can play against type.

ALEC: John and Della are a nurse and an old guy in a wheelchair. I think Della should be the guy. Who painted these sets? They're crap.

SAM: They're from last year. *The Indelible Mr. Sprocket.*

ALEC: The robot musical.

SAM: Yeah.

ALEC: Were you in that? Oh—sorry, I didn't see it.

SAM: Yeah.

ALEC: I can't see any play about robots.

SAM: Like the instruction manuals. You can't stand machines getting along by themselves.

Alec touches the tip of his nose and winks.

ALEC: You were really good in *Oklahoma!*

SAM: Thanks.

ALEC: No, really.

SAM: Thanks, really.

ALEC: I thought it was going to suck ass.

SAM: It's a lot of corn.

ALEC: But it had a kind of a good, old-timey feel to it. The corn.

SAM: It was as high as an elephant's eye.

ALEC: You did a great job. You really got into it.

SAM: I was as high as an elephant's eye.

ALEC (*briefly a Hollywood director*): You were bigger than that play, baby. I'm going to make you a star.

SAM: Don't say that while you're lying on the casting couch. I might just . . .

That's just awkward enough that they don't know what to say now.

SAM (*to disturb the silence*): Have you ever been in a play?

ALEC: Yeah. A role-play about camping safety.

SAM: That sounds incredible.

ALEC: *The Times* raved, but it flopped in Europe.

SAM: So why are you taking this class?

ALEC: Four months to graduation. I've suddenly become real interested in drama and pottery.

SAM: Do you know where you're going?

ALEC: Whichever school opens their arms and shakes their *boozoms*. I didn't apply anywhere early decision. You know yet?

SAM: Yeah. But I oddly enough am taking the class because I like acting.

ALEC: You're good at it.

Pause.

SAM: Thanks.

ALEC: I don't have any natural talent for it except my rugged good looks and my incredible fucking charm.

Pause. A little awkward. Alec gets up again and surveys the set.

ALEC: How long are we supposed to improv?

SAM: Until we've come up with material.

ALEC: What's material?

SAM: A situation.

ALEC: That's a little vague.

SAM: A conflict.

ALEC: Why do we keep this picture up, darling? We look awful. It's totally unflattering. We look like fucking manatees. I mean, except, of course, honey darling, you look like the most beautiful manatee in the world.

SAM: Sure. Sailors mistake me for mermaids.

ALEC: Are we going to the Higginses' on Saturday? Marty Higgins sent us an invite. I'm assuming we'll go.

SAM: Sure.

ALEC: Why don't you disagree with me?

SAM: Why? I love the Higginses. Jessica cracks me up.

ALEC: Conflict.

SAM: We're great at parties. We're a hit. (*She thinks.*) Well, you are.

ALEC: I am. It's true. I tell a good story. I can put away whisky sours with the best of them. You're shy, but I always draw you into the story.

SAM: You wear a blue blazer, don't you?

ALEC: I do. I have a lot of stories to tell. I'm a prominent spy. The ladies love me.

SAM: You're a hedge-fund manager.

ALEC: I say prominent spy.

SAM: No one's a prominent spy.

ALEC: I am. You would not believe the shit my car does. Hovercraft is the fucking least of it.

SAM: A spy can't be prominent.

ALEC: Yes, they can.

SAM: A prominent spy can't spy anymore. A prominent spy is a crappy spy.

ALEC: Oh, touché, Miss Moneypenny.

SAM: I'm just saying.

ALEC: Was that a conflict?

SAM: That was pathetic.

ALEC: I'm working on it. Are you going to the graduation party at Trent's out in Vegas?

SAM: Yeah.

ALEC: It's going to be off the leash.

SAM: No. Because we're going to find out Trent doesn't really live in Vegas. He lives somewhere in the desert about an hour or two away from Vegas. It's completely desolate. It's somewhere near Death Valley.

ALEC: So do we end up going, honey? Do we remember it years later? Oh, the good times. We tell the kids about it.

SAM: Yeah, we remember it. It was amazing. We were driving along the highway and the heat was rolling in through the windows. It was less like air and more like Oriental carpets. Big, hot folds. Heaped up, you know? And you're in the middle of nowhere and all there is is a restaurant called the Bun Boy with a giant rectal thermometer sticking out of it reading a hundred fifteen degrees Fahrenheit. And there we were, going down the highway, speeding, the way we're supposed to be when we've just graduated.

ALEC: I guess Farooq wasn't fucking driving. That kid would rather take a bullet than break the speed limit.

SAM: It's required you speed after graduation.

ALEC: So someone can wrap tragically around a tree?

SAM: There weren't any trees. It's Death Valley. The speeding's so you can feel full of life and change. And so you can hold your arms out the window, and all the hairs on our arms were sticking straight out because of some weird static electricity thing, and for a minute, our bare arms rubbed together—I mean, yours and mine—and I'd had a crush on you all through high school—and there were our arms, touching—and I thought, *Whoa. This is it. I'm alive.*

ALEC: And then—okay, get this—and then we got lost, the whole carload of us, and someone—Melissa—she freaked, and screamed, "We're in Death Valley and we don't know where we're going," and this was so fucking funny that we all started to chant, "We're lost in the Valley of Death! And we don't know where we're going! We don't know where we're going!"

SAM (*pointing*): Cute! . . . Symbolic!

ALEC: And there we were, driving through the night, thinking we didn't know where we were going, but over us there was a whole, like, a whole big, flat, desert sky for us to drive into, and any direction we could go. Any direction at all. Pick one and you'll end up someplace. Nothing *can fucking hold us back, man!*

SAM: Well done.

ALEC: Thank you.

SAM: It's perfect.

ALEC: So is that when we got together?

SAM: No. We were just friends through college. I didn't see you for like two years. Then there was a party at

Bonnie's on Nantucket. It was amazing. I hate Bonnie's music collection—it sucks—but she had Bill Derringer do the music, and we were all dancing in the saw grass. We didn't even realize until later that our legs were getting all cut up. Someone was making chocolate margaritas and we both got totally drunk off our asses and late that night we started making out. God, it was incredible. The light in the morning was amazing. We kept looking around and we couldn't believe how vivid everything in the world was. Every blade of grass had a shadow. And there we were, together. Unfortunately, you'd been so drunk you didn't remember any of it. I was too shy to tell you. I drove back to school and cried for about a week. But after that we started to send each other messages all the time. You asked my advice about all the girls you went out with. Once while one of them was doing you. You kept up this monologue.

ALEC: Okay. This is getting a little weird.

SAM (*shrugs*): You asked.

ALEC: You know I have a girlfriend.

SAM: Yeah. Right now.

ALEC: Okay. Let's move on.

SAM: The summer of our junior year in college, we went with Bill and about four other people to China. We finally did it in Gansu. I mean, made love. We hadn't taken a bath for about three days. There was something incredibly human about the way we smelled.

ALEC: All right. Okay. Fine. You're freaking me out.

SAM: Sorry. I can't believe you don't remember.

ALEC: Ha-ha.

SAM: I'm sorry, Alec.

ALEC (*somehow uncomfortable that she's using his name*): Sure. Whatever.

SAM: I'm really sorry. I don't mean to scare you.

ALEC: Yeah. Look—jokes aside—there's Madison. And it's weird.

SAM: Okay.

ALEC: Okay. Thanks.

An awkward pause.

SAM (*trying to reestablish their rhythm and banter from before. She points out the window to the nonexistent neighbors*): Jed McMasters takes you heli-skiing. You know, drops you in the mountains and you ski down.

Alec, unwilling to play, just nods.

SAM: Have you seen Jed in the city recently?

ALEC: No.

SAM: Too bad.

ALEC: Yeah.

SAM: It's not often you meet someone with a helicopter *and* an airplane.

ALEC: No.

SAM: He's gone, I think.

ALEC: Oh.

SAM: He and Greta were at a party, and while Greta was off talking to someone, he met this beautiful Russian woman who said she wanted to go home to St. Petersburg. So he told her he had his pilot's license and he'd take her. Boom. Gone. Off they flew. Leaving Greta alone.

ALEC: Too bad.

SAM: Yeah. Greta had to get a ride home.

ALEC: You mean, he took off right from the party? He flew to St. Petersburg from the party?

SAM: Yeah.

ALEC: Your material is starting to suck.

SAM: It sounded kind of *Great Gatsby* to me.

ALEC: Okay. I've had enough. What's our situation?

SAM: You're not even playing along anymore.

ALEC: I'll play along if we can just decide what our fucking situation is.

SAM: We're supposed to feel it out.

ALEC: Don't say things like "feel it out."

SAM (*teasing*): Here's what happened. I'd had a crush on you through high school. I finally told you in China. And the rest is history.

ALEC: See? Stop it. What's our actual situation? And what are these fucking machines?

SAM: They create images. Projections. Sounds. That's our situation.

ALEC: Why is that our situation?

SAM: Because you're a projection.

ALEC: You're kind of fucked up.

SAM: That's also part of our situation. I'm grieving.

ALEC: Let's talk about something normal. Do we come back for alumni weekends? Yes. Yes, we do.

SAM: You know what's depressing? Each time we go back—ten, twenty, twenty-five, fifty—

ALEC: Fifty? Shit.

SAM: Each time, we keep hoping the beautiful people will look decrepit and awful. Paunches. Jowls. Bellies. But that's the problem with going to a private school. Years pass, and everyone's still beautiful. They have too much money to age badly.

ALEC: Jesus Christ. I think you're right. The bastards. At least I'll retain my boyish good looks.

SAM: If you say so.

ALEC: That doesn't sound good.

SAM: You might get a turkey wobble. A little turkey wobble. Don't worry about it.

ALEC (*protecting his neck*): No way. I've seen those alumni staggering around the campus. No fucking way. (*Dodders.*) *"I say, Jeffers, 'twasn't it in the belfry that we buggered O'Shaunessy?"*

Sam laughs.

ALEC: *"Is that the library? . . . Near the dining hall? . . . I wonder whether they still have God in the chapel. In my day, there was a God in the chapel. Remember? Crucified chap."*

SAM: Each time, we drive there joking about how people will have lost some of their youthful energy. Then we get there and they're all doing great. They're all headed off to invest in dude ranches in Venezuela. It's incredibly depressing. We drive home in hysterics.

ALEC: They must have slowed down by the fiftieth.

SAM (*a little reluctant*): You don't . . . You aren't there at the fiftieth. You don't . . . You haven't made it.

ALEC: I'm a very active man.

SAM: A lot of people start getting cancer. A lot.

ALEC: I'm extremely hearty. I go heli-skiing with Jed McMasters.

SAM: You work out all the time. You take the kids swimming when they're younger. Yeah, sure, and skiing, and we go hiking.

ALEC: So why are you killing me off?

Pause.

SAM: I'm sorry, Alec.

ALEC: Wait. Why do you get to say what I do, *honey?* You seem to have a lot of opinions about that, *honey.* Well, I'm a fucking prominent spy, and I don't take any shit. That whole hedge-fund-manager thing is a ruse, *darling.* We can decide together about where we're going for vacation or what sofa to get or what little Jimmy gets for his *allowance,* but thank you very fucking much, I think I get to decide when I *die.*

The room seems chilly, sad, and fragile.

SAM: You do, in a way. (*Pause.*) Before you do, you sit down and record your persona. You have an imprint taken. In your will, you tell me how to access it. The imprint. You tell me I can have you with me whenever I want. Projected.

ALEC: I don't get it.

SAM: A few months before you died.

ALEC: So it is up to you to decide when I died.

SAM: You decided when you died.

ALEC: Thank you.

SAM: I knew the night before . . . I mean, one way or the other, it was only a matter of weeks. Because of the cancer. (*Increasingly in a reverie.*) That night, I was almost out of your hospital room, and you called me back. I shut the door and came back to your bedside and you said you wanted to hold my hand. We held hands. Then you smiled and said thank you, and I started to leave, and just as I was almost out the door, you called me back again. You said you wanted me to hold you. So I came back and held you. I mean, as well as I could. There were wires and tubes. And then I said not to worry, I'd be back the next day, and you said you knew. And I went outside and started walking down the hall, and I heard you calling me back again, so I went in, and you said you wanted to hold my hand again. That was when I knew you were going. (*Pause.*) Or that's how I remember it now. Maybe I didn't know. I'm not sure how I couldn't know. I wouldn't have left if I'd known. . . . Right? . . . Anyway, I left and came back the next day to read with you. Then they told me. I . . . didn't . . .

ALEC: Don't tell me about this.

SAM: I'm sorry. What do you want to talk about?

ALEC: I don't care.

SAM: What do you want to know?

ALEC: Anything. I don't know. About the kids.

SAM: They're wonderful kids, Alec. Sometimes they're here. Two of them. Five grandchildren. Two of the grandchildren die of the cancer. Suresh, the oldest of the grandkids, is going to Juilliard. Piano. (*Lovingly.*) He's as handsome as you, and as charming, but not as much of an asshole.

ALEC: I don't understand. Is this supposed to be the situation?

SAM: It is the situation, Alec. It's always the situation.

ALEC: The situation is you sitting here in a room alone. And everything looks how it used to. And I'm just a figment of your imagination.

SAM: No. You're a figment of your own imagination, recorded. You have responses. They're reconstructed. But yes, everything looks how it looked, while the machines run. I look how I looked. You look how you looked.

ALEC: And the machine stores all my memories.

SAM: No. You didn't record the two years you lived with Greta McMasters. You were too kind to let me know what that was like.

ALEC: So all my memories are yours. My whole life is about you.

SAM: No. They're your memories. They're yours. Your persona is reconstructed. Just like you wanted. Whenever I wish. Sometimes it's Christmas. Sometimes we talk about the kids, nothing but the kids. Sometimes we're on vacation, in Thailand or Cambodia. The kids are teenagers again. Petra's about to graduate. Or Petra's pregnant with Suresh, calling on the phone and begging us for furniture. (*Pause.*) Sometimes I sit by you while you're dying. When you ask me to come back and hold your hand, I don't leave. Not immediately. But sooner or later, I have to get up and go. . . . This time I know. I know that you're not going to be there when I get back. But I can't sit there forever. I have to let you do what you did. . . . (*Pause.*) Sometimes we're having breakfast. Sometimes we're making up stories about people, just like this. It's something we always return to. Sometimes we're making love, but I can't feel anything. You don't have any weight, you're on top of me, groaning, but you don't have—

ALEC: Okay. You're freaking me out.

SAM: —you don't have any substance, and I'm trying to hold on to you, and I can't, because there's nothing there but light.

ALEC: Stop it.

SAM: And sometimes—

ALEC: I swear to fucking god, stop it.

SAM: Sometimes we're having the first conversation we ever had—the first real conversation—about an assignment where we have to improv that we're married. We're back at the beginning.

ALEC: You are so fucked up it's not even funny.

SAM: And it's my dream, because I've had a crush on you for at least two years.

ALEC: You are so fucked up. Okay. It's over!

SAM: I can't talk like a girl anymore. I know too much. I'm seventy, and still sad.

ALEC: You're so fucked up.

SAM: Your middle name is Dwight. Your parents' house

is in Canaan, Massachusetts. Your father has an airbrush painting of a blond woman Rollerblading on the wall of his home office, which drives you crazy. When you were thirteen and you had a party, you covered the picture with a blanket because you were so embarrassed by it. Your little sister, Sylvia, was born with a harelip, now almost invisible. She calls you "Gaddy." Your first kiss—

ALEC: Holy shit. You are a complete stalker.

SAM: I'm not a stalker, Alec. I'm sorry. The pretense is over. I can't stand this.

ALEC: You are insane. Fucking insane!

SAM: I can almost never get through a scene with you without—

ALEC: Scene's over.

SAM (*as if to a dead man, via his live image*): Alec, I love you. I loved you. I loved you.

ALEC: It's over! I'm done! I'll take the F, thanks!

SAM: I loved you. . . . I miss you. . . . I miss you.

ALEC: I'm leaving now. (*Heads for the door.*)

SAM: Honey, don't.

ALEC: Don't fucking "honey" me, you insane bitch.

SAM: When you walk out of the door, you'll cease. There's no environment there.

ALEC: I'll fucking cease all the way up to Daley's office and tell him I'm not working with you.

SAM (*desperate*): Alec, I'm sorry. I'm sorry. I'll stop.

ALEC: You're fucking insane. Stop talking to me. Stop stalking me.

SAM: I'll stop whatever you tell me to stop.

ALEC: You need help. I'm not trying to be mean.

SAM: You'd never be mean, Alec. The kids—when the kids were little—

ALEC: Fuck you! Fuck you!

SAM (*a threat*): You can go if you want to. I'll just reconstitute you again.

ALEC: *INSANE!*

SAM (*desperately*): I'm sorry. I didn't mean that. I'm not telling you that. Go. You're just a kid.

ALEC: Of course I'm just a fucking kid! Of course I'm just a fucking kid!

SAM: And we're going to go to a party, a graduation party, and driving—we'll be driving down the road, and we don't know where we're going. And we're sitting there, and I'm looking around at us and we're all young, and I wonder how we'll teach ourselves ever to be grown-up, and I wonder whether we have our deaths curled up in us already, waiting to bloom, and our fates, like ferns, and we don't know, so—

ALEC: This is all *bullshit* because I would never go out with you in a thousand *years,* and I would never fuck you in China, and I'll never make out with you in Nantucket, because you're a crazy, drug-addicted bitch and *fuck you.*

Sam weeps.

SAM: Our whole lives were ahead of us. That's the saying. Our whole lives.

ALEC. And for the record, I made up the part about us getting lost. That was me.

SAM: I know.

ALEC: So don't go saying it's real.

SAM: I know.

ALEC: I'm completely out of your league. Try this on one of your acting buddies. You can work out a whole "situation." If one of them by accident isn't gay.

SAM: Fuck you.

ALEC: That's right.

SAM: No, fuck you. Fuck you, Alec.

ALEC: That's right.

SAM (*weeping*): Fuck you for making the imprint.

ALEC: Jesus Christ.

SAM: Fuck you for never dying. Fuck you for never dying, so I can never grieve over you, but I can keep replaying each scene, and keep wrecking them like this because I want you to be here—fully here—fully knowing—fully who you will be—not some kid—or some young father—but the man I lived with for thirty-six years—and so I can't stop seeing you—and I can't stop telling you—and now I don't even have my own memories—because all I remember now are a series of these fucking scenes where we start and it's like it was and then I try to tell you—like an idiot—and you—of course—you—

ALEC: Walk out.

SAM: Sometimes. Sometimes. Sometimes you don't. I can hardly remember what happened before you were just an image. And I've never grieved, and I've never lost you, and I'm always losing you.

ALEC: Right now.

SAM: I've lost you.

ALEC: Right now.

SAM: There's so much possibility. Originally, we didn't argue. I didn't tell you you couldn't be a spy. Our deaths aren't with us yet, Alec. Nothing's decided.

ALEC: It's decided.

SAM: For the moment. Until I turn on the machine again.

ALEC: See you at *lunch*.

SAM: Sure, Alec.

ALEC: At *lunch*. Out the fucking *door*.

SAM: Sure.

Alec leaves.

For a long time, Sam sits silently.

SAM (*announcing, as if to no one*): All right. That's all. I'm done. That's the situation. I'm done.

There's a long silence again. She gets up and leaves. She flicks a switch by the door. It must be a light switch. At least, the lights go out.

The end.

Deborah Noyes

M. T. Anderson is the author of many critically acclaimed picture books and novels, including *Thirsty, Burger Wuss, Feed,* which was a National Book Award finalist and the winner of the *Los Angeles Times* Book Prize, and *The Astonishing Life of Octavian Nothing, Traitor to the Nation Vol. 1: The Pox Party,* which won a National Book Award and was a Michael L. Printz Honor Book. His picture books include *Handel, Who Know What He Liked,* illustrated by Kevin Hawkes, and *The Serpent Came to Gloucester,* illustrated by Bagram Ibatoulline. Additionally, he is the author of the M. T. Anderson's Thrilling Tales series, which includes *Whales on Stilts* and *The Clue of the Linoleum Lederhosen.* He lives outside Boston, Massachusetts.

Survival

K. L. Going

 In twenty minutes I will stand before my graduating class and give the class president's speech honoring our years of hard work and achievement. I've chosen as my theme "Surviving High School."

In five minutes my classmates and I will file onto the football field under a cloudless blue sky, a spectacle of bright green gowns and tasseled caps. Our friends and family will stand to applaud this, the crowning achievement of our adolescence. One moment in time, eighteen years in the making.

In one minute I will take my place in line, waiting to hear the command that will start our procession forward. My palms will be sweaty and my breath will be short. I will shut my eyes and go numb.

In *this* moment, I am watching my older sister kiss the only boy I've ever loved under the Thomas Jefferson High School bleachers.

Sarah

When we were little, my sister Sarah was a twirler. She was always wearing something sparkly that flowed around her in waves, and now as I look back, I wonder if she chose those things herself, even at ages three, four, and five, or whether Mom and Dad made an unconscious decision to stack her wardrobe with clothes that would catch the light.

My clothes were colorful sometimes, with cool decals and maybe fun stitching, but next to Sarah's they were flat and dull.

Once, when I was four, I asked Sarah to teach me how to twirl the way she did.

"Please?"

She put her hands on her hips and stuck out her stomach the way only a seven-year-old would.

"No."

"Please, Sarah? Please, please, *pleeeease?*"

"You won't do it right."

"How come?"

"Because you have to be grown up like me."

"But why?"

"'Cause when you're grown up, you're smarter and prettier and everyone loves you more. When you're little, you can't do anything."

"Nuh-uh!"

"Yuh-huh. You can't twirl. Only I can do it. See?"

Sarah held her hands up high over her head like a ballerina and twirled around the living room. Her long blond hair, unbrushed, swirled around her face, and her blue jeans with the sequined butterflies on the back pockets sparkled like diamonds. She looked *exactly* like a ballerina.

"I'm going to do it too," I said.

I put my hands up over my head, but they felt awkward, like they weren't really part of my body. What should I do with them?

I studied Sarah's hands, the exact way she held them in little water-fountain arcs, so they bent together, pinkies extended, and I tried to copy the way that they looked. Then I launched myself forward, feeling the momentum take me, the dizziness rushing in.

Now I'm twirling, I thought, *and next time Grammy and Grampy come over, I'll show them how I can do it the same way as Sarah and they'll clap for me just like they clap for her.*

I went faster and faster, the light from the bay window making patterns behind my closed eyelids every time I passed by. The world was moving in circles, coming unglued.

Then I heard a crash and my mother's footsteps rushed in from the kitchen.

"Girls! What are you doing?"

As I slowed, she came into focus, a blurry figure kneeling next to the shards of colored glass that lay beside the living room hutch. At first the scene wouldn't stay still, but finally it stopped, and I could see that her face was knotted and her lip was quivering just like mine did when I tried not to cry. My eyes were wide.

"Your father gave me this on our first anniversary. It was . . ."

I knew it had been her favorite. Daddy always said, "Beautiful, just like your mother" when he held it up to the light. I'd stroked it many times, always so careful.

"Who broke this?"

My heart beat fast. Had I done it?

Sarah pointed at me.

"Rachel," my mother said, "go to your room."

Like an explosion, I burst into tears of guilt and remorse, but Mom just shook her head. I knelt on the floor and grabbed one big chunk of glass that had scattered under the rocking chair. It was the lady's legs from the knees down. For a moment I thought maybe the figurine could be glued and everything could be fixed, but there were no more large chunks. The rest of the glass was broken into tiny shards and some of those were ground into the living room floor as if a sneaker had trampled them.

Sarah's feet were right next to the shards of glass, and she was wearing sneakers with red glittery swirls on them. I was wearing plain brown socks.

I cried harder. "Mom, Sarah did it!"

My mother grabbed my elbow.

"Not another word out of you, young lady. I told you to go to your room." She pulled me hard, which wasn't like my mom at all. Mom was soft, gentle. Except today she was crying, and no matter how hard she pulled at my sleeve, seeing her tears was worse.

"I told you not to play next to the hutch," she said, wiping her cheek with the back of her hand. "How many times do I have to tell you girls, no twirling in the living room?"

But I had never twirled. Not once until today.

Mom ushered me into my room and I collapsed on my spaceship quilt.

"Ten-minute time-out," she said, shutting the door behind her. "Then we will talk about this."

I sobbed for a long time, then breathed in hard gulps. My eyes stung. I lay still and wondered . . . had I done it or had Sarah lied?

I tried to remember exactly where I'd twirled. Had I gotten close to the hutch? Had my elbow grazed the edge, causing it to shake, so the figure had fallen and smashed? I remembered the stomach-churning pull of the dizziness. I'd closed my eyes and hadn't watched where I was going.

But Sarah had sneakers on. I didn't. She was the one next to the hutch.

I pictured her face as she pointed, her blue eyes solemn, staring straight at me. Then I pulled my stuffed unicorn close and buried my head in my pillow. *I will never grow up*, I vowed, repeating the words like a mantra. *Being grown up is stupid and I won't ever do it, even if it means I never get to twirl again.*

But in my mind I heard Sarah's words again. *". . . when you're grown up, you're smarter and prettier and everyone loves you more. When you're little, you can't do anything."*

And I wondered . . . was she right?

Kenneth

The first time I met Kenneth, we were freshmen and I was doubled over, gasping for air. My face was bright red, the way it always got when I ran, and sweat was dripping down my neck, through my shirt, and into the sports bra that was flattening my already flat chest. Not exactly a shining moment, except I'd just run 5:42 in our first timed 1500-meter and Coach was impressed.

"Not bad, Rachel. By the time you're a junior, you'll be one of our top competitors." He turned to the next group of girls and gave the signal to start. I was grateful for the break. I considered collapsing on the grass in an undignified heap, but someone reached over and handed me a water bottle.

"That was awesome," a voice said from slightly behind me.

I took the water bottle and drank, unable to stifle my smile.

"Kenneth Fisher," the boy said, extending his hand. "School newspaper."

"Rachel Greeley."

Kenneth had tufty dark brown hair and eyes that were deep set, as if he hadn't gotten any sleep the night before, only you could tell that was the way they looked all the time. He was thin and wiry, a classic geek, yet there was something about him that made me flush.

"You're a freshman too, right?" he asked.

I nodded, straightening.

"I remember you from the all-state track meet last

year. I went to Hillsborough Middle School and covered it for the school paper."

"Really?" I said, finally able to breathe normally again.

"Yeah. My family moved here this past summer just in time for me to start high school knowing exactly no one."

I laughed, but Kenneth was squinting at me.

"You won the fifteen-hundred-meter, right? I watched that race."

"Mmm-hmm."

It was hard to believe anyone would remember me.

"You beat out one of our best competitors by a fraction of a second."

"Oh," I said. "Sorry."

Kenneth laughed. "Don't be sorry. Have you been running your whole life?"

I shook my head. "Hardly. I used to play tennis, only last year I switched to track instead."

Kenneth took this in, but he didn't ask the obvious question. Why switch in eighth grade? I could tell he wasn't truly in reporter mode. He was interested in me.

Even so, I thought about the years I'd spent playing tennis. Waiting outside the chain-link fence until I was big enough to hold a racket and play on the court with the older girls. The hours spent mimicking everything Sarah did, trying so hard to catch up to her.

I was good, too. You always are when you want something bad enough.

Kenneth ran a hand in front of my face.

"Earth to Rachel. You okay?"

I took a deep breath. "Of course. Let's go sit on the bleachers before Coach calls me up again."

I took off and Kenneth followed. There was something easy about him, as if we were already good friends even though we'd just met. When we got to the bleachers, he leaned back, feet up on the shiny metal riser in front of us, elbows propped on the riser in back. He looked comfortable, and without thinking about it, I eased myself next to him.

"So, you probably know all these people, right?" he asked.

I looked around at the rest of the track team milling around below, some stretching, some making their way around the track, some looking lost, the way I usually did.

"Not really," I admitted. "I mean I know who most of them are, but it's hard to join a sport late. Everyone already has their friends, you know?"

"Oh, yes," Kenneth said, serious with a touch of self-mockery. "I know *very* well. But at least you know their names. It's hard to write a story about the track season kickoff when you don't know who anyone is. So tell me, who's that guy doing the long jump? And the girl with the braided hair?"

"Dave Ratchet and Kylie Anderson. Dave's the hottie everyone lusts after and Kylie is the girl everyone is afraid of."

"And the redhead over there?"

"Claire Witherspoon, who claims she's related to Reese Witherspoon, only no one believes her."

"The guy with the Mohawk?"

"Duane Right. Nice guy, but I can't figure out how he ended up on the team."

Kenneth laughed.

"You're good at this." He paused and looked around.

"How about . . ." His eyes lingered for a long time—so long, I thought he might have forgotten all about our game. "Her . . ." he said at last, too casually. "The beautiful one with the long blond hair?"

I followed his finger with my eyes.

"Which one?"

"The one who's about to finish first."

"That's . . ." I stood up. "Damn it."

Kenneth was sitting up straight now.

"You guys enemies or something?"

I could feel the tears stinging my eyes and had to fight to keep them back.

"No," I spat. "We're sisters."

Below, Sarah was finishing her race and Coach was grinning from ear to ear. I could barely hear his voice in the distance, like a radio whose dial was turned way down.

"That's a new record for this team," he was saying. "I knew we could make a star out of you if you finally gave track a try. I never thought I'd convince you, Sarah, but I can tell this is going to be a great year."

A great year?

Leaving Kenneth behind, I walked down from the bleachers onto the field, my legs like Jell-O.

I will not cry, I promised myself over and over again, but the moment I was next to her, the tears threatened to spill out.

"What are you doing here?" I choked.

Sarah looked up as if she were surprised. Who knows . . . maybe she really was. It was always hard to tell with Sarah. She had a way of widening her eyes with what you believed could only be true shock. Until you saw that same expression over again and over again, and you began to wonder.

"Coach has been asking me to join since I was a freshman," she said, "and my tennis elbow has been getting worse, so I said yes. What's your problem?"

What was my problem? I wanted to say a thousand things.

My problem is that you come in like a steamroller, plowing over everything in your path until you get what you want, and if you want to be the star of the track team before you graduate high school, then you'll do it and I'll spend the rest of my four years on the team being referred to as Sarah's sister.

My problem is that there are at least five other sports you're good at, but you just happened to choose this one?

My problem is that you think about no one other than yourself.

But of course nothing that coherent came out of my mouth.

"Track is *my* thing," I said, sputtering. "You've got tennis."

Sarah put her hands on her hips. "I don't get you, Rachel," she said with the superior tone of voice she always used when we were fighting. "Track isn't *yours*. You can't claim something belongs to you when it doesn't. I wanted to join track, so I did. It's got nothing to do with you, so just grow up."

This was Sarah's signature line—the one I'd been hearing since I was born.

Grow up.

By now there was a small crowd of people trying to pretend they weren't watching us, but I knew what they were thinking.

We need Sarah so we'll have a winning season. How can Rachel be so selfish?

I bit my lip and turned away, walking blindly back toward the bleachers, wondering if the snickers I heard were real or imaginary. I'm not sure what I would have done next . . . maybe I'd have wandered aimlessly off the field and given up on track too. But that's when I felt a hand on my shoulder.

Kenneth. I'd forgotten all about him.

"Hey, wait up," he said, slowing me down.

Tears were slipping down my cheeks. I couldn't look at Kenneth, so I didn't turn around, but I did stop walking and wiped my face with my hands.

"That was a shitty thing to do," he said, and I nodded. He was right. I shouldn't have confronted Sarah. How could I stand in the way of what she wanted?

"I know," I whispered. "I . . ."

"I mean your sister," he said. "I didn't know she was your sister when I asked about her, but I did know who she was," he confessed. "I asked Marcus Winthrop about her yesterday, and he said she's the best tennis player this school has ever had. I'd say that leaving the sport you're great at in order to be great at the same sport your little sister just happens to be awesome at is . . . well, it's shitty, that's all."

I barely knew this guy, but it took every ounce of strength not to throw my arms around him. My heart sped up in a way that it had never done before, and my breathing was shallow, but this time it was not from my run.

Could this be it?

After years of thinking I couldn't fall in love the way Sarah did—years of worrying that I was broken—was this finally it?

Please God, I begged. *Let this be it.*

What I didn't let myself think about was the way Kenneth looked back at the field—at Sarah—long and hard before he walked away with me.

Sarah

"Come on, tell me."

It was May, and Sarah was sitting cross-legged on my beanbag chair holding a magazine, watching me over the edge of the pages. It was two weeks before her graduation, and everyone she knew must have been busy or else she wouldn't have been hanging out here, in my room. "You've got to like someone," she said, raising one eyebrow.

I stopped reorganizing my bookshelf and thought of Kenneth. *Pined* would be a better word. Longed for. Gazed at from a distance.

Actually, the distance part wasn't quite true. He was my best friend, so I saw him up close and personal all the time. I just hadn't told him how I felt.

I wasn't about to tell Sarah first.

"There's no one," I said. "What about you?"

Sarah sat up straighter and her eyes sparkled.

"Do you really want to know?"

Actually, the question should have been did she really want to tell me? Apparently, she did.

"Sure."

"I've met my soul mate." She leaned back and let the magazine fall open across her chest.

"I've heard that before," I said, rolling my eyes, but Sarah only threw the magazine at me across the room.

"This time I mean it," she said. "His name's Jordan

and I met him at the mall. He's so amazing, Rachel. Tall, blond, gorgeous. He says we're meant for each other."

"Does he go to Thomas Jefferson?" I asked, trying to think of a single guy named Jordan in Sarah's senior class.

"Not exactly," she said, her face morphing into a mask of innocence.

I set down the volume of Emily Dickinson's poetry that I was about to shelve.

"What do you mean, not exactly?"

"He's older."

"How much older?"

"Twenty-one."

"Sarah, you have got to be kidding me! Mom and Dad will freak out."

"*Shhhh,*" she said, glancing at my bedroom door, which was already shut. "They don't need to know yet. Promise you won't tell." She waited a moment while I took a deep breath, then said, "Rachel, *promise.*"

"All right, all right. I promise."

Satisfied, Sarah leaned back again.

"He looks kind of like Brad Pitt," she said, laughing.

"I'm going to go all the way with him."

"Sarah!"

"Quiet!"

"You can't."

"Why not?"

"Because you're . . . well . . . you're still in high school and he's . . ."

"Oh, grow up, Rachel. Everyone has sex in high school."

Did they?

I hadn't even kissed anyone yet. Sure, there were the obligatory closed-lipped pecks during spin-the-bottle games at Lisa Maller's birthday parties, but who counted those? Before long, I'd be sixteen—the first sixteen-year-old since 1930 who could honestly say she'd never been kissed.

Sarah studied me.

"You haven't done anything yet, have you?" she said, secure in the knowledge that she was right. I thought about lying, but one of the annoying things about an older sister is that she can almost always tell when you're fibbing.

"I thought we were talking about you," I said, but now Sarah's interest was piqued.

"You haven't given a guy a blow job?"

I couldn't disguise the expression that flashed across my face.

"God no!"

Sarah laughed.

"It's not that bad," she said. "Plenty of people do it."

"Well, not me."

"French kissed, then?"

Honestly, French kissing sounded just as gross as blow jobs—all that awful bodily fluid involved—but this time I turned away just as my cheeks caught fire.

"Oh my Lord, you haven't? Regular kissing then? Tell me you have kissed *some*body, right? You're going to be a sophomore soon, Rachel. Don't tell me you haven't . . ."

"Shut up," I said, picking up the magazine and throwing it back at her. I threw it hard and it smacked her in the face, though I hadn't meant it to.

"Bitch," she said, "why do you have to get so defensive?"

"Why do you have to act like I'm a freak just because I'm not . . . you?"

"Because you're still such a baby."

"At least I'm not out there giving blow jobs to guys at the mall I hardly even know!"

"You're such a brat," Sarah said, breathless. "I told you we're soul mates." She got up and pushed me hard with both hands so I fell back against my bookshelf.

I struggled to my feet and pushed her back.

Sarah kicked me in the shin.

Then before I knew it, we were grappling, just like we had as kids, my hands tugging at Sarah's sweatshirt and her fingers looped in my hair, pulling hard. I let out a yell.

"I hate you."

It was a strangled cry that came from somewhere deep within me, and Sarah let go, backing up and panting hard.

"You are a freak," she said. "I can't wait to graduate and get out of this place. Jordan and I are moving to California and I'm never coming back. I hate it here. I've always hated it here. I'm getting out of this hellhole the minute I've got my diploma."

I was glaring at her with all my might.

"Do you think I care?" I said, but of course I was lying, and Sarah knew it.

"Someday you're going to see what the world is really like, Rachel. It isn't Mom and Dad and Thomas Jefferson High School, that's for sure. And it isn't your nerdy GPA or your stupid Emily Dickinson poetry."

She kicked the volume so hard that it slid across my hardwood floor.

"So what is it then?" I spat.

Sarah looked at me as if I were the lowest creature on the food chain.

"You won't understand until you grow up," she said. Then she turned and walked out of my room, slamming the door behind her.

Kenneth

"Graduation is going to change everything," Kenneth said, leaning back on the bleachers in our favorite spot. It was the last day of our first week as sophomores, and I was contemplating life without Sarah now that she'd left for college in California, and Kenneth was contemplating life without high school.

"Everything will be so perfect once we're finally out of this dump. Did you know there are only 536 school days left until it's our turn?"

This was the first of what would be many subsequent announcements.

"Is that meant to be depressing?" I asked. "Because it sure doesn't sound encouraging when you put it that way."

Kenneth calculated again, his brain working at feverish speed.

"That's 12,864 hours of real time and 4,288 hours of school time. Give or take a few snow days and two-hour delays."

"You're insane."

Kenneth grinned back at me, and my heart did its familiar somersault.

"It's never too early to start the countdown."

I wondered if that was true, and my mind flashed back to Sarah again. Counting down toward *what*? Apparently Kenneth's mind had also flashed to Sarah, because he put his chin in his hands and frowned.

"Sarah is so lucky she's out of here. UC Berkeley is a great school. I would totally consider going there. . . ."

I groaned. Kenneth was way too smart for Berkeley, and everyone knew it but him. He was meant for Harvard or Yale or MIT.

"Does she like it so far?" he asked.

"College?"

"Yeah."

I shrugged.

"When's she coming home?"

"Who knows?" I picked at the frayed edge of my shoelace.

"Well, does she seem happy now that she's away? She told me once that she wanted to be . . . you know . . . free."

He sounded so uncomfortable, I laughed. Kenneth was far too practical to say melodramatic things like *she wanted to be free* without blushing.

"I really don't know," I said, and that was the truth. Was Sarah happy? She was in perpetual motion, always going someplace or doing something. Madly in love and then tragically heartbroken. In pursuit. Twirling.

But did that make her happy?

"I've never known," I said.

Kenneth nodded. "It will make *me* happy when *I* can leave." He said it so seriously, my eyebrows shot up.

"Really?" I asked, wondering why the rush. "Then tell me . . . what are you looking forward to the most?"

This time it was Kenneth's turn to laugh. "God, what am I *not* looking forward to?" he said, but then he stopped and thought about my question. "The demise of sixth-period study hall," he announced. "That's what I'm most looking forward to."

"Well, you won't have to wait until graduation for that. You'll have a new schedule next year."

Kenneth frowned. "I meant it symbolically, Rach. As long as we're in high school, there will always be a sixth-period study hall." He fixed me with a meaningful stare. "You know what I'm talking about—a class where the teacher looks the other way while guys like Bart Sanders steal the economics report you worked on for a week right before the class where it's due. Tell me . . . when does that happen in the real world? No one waits around in the hallway to intimidate adults by stealing their work and calling them 'faggot.'"

I supposed he must have a point. That stuff couldn't continue happening after high school, could it?

"It's totally ironic," Kenneth added, "because guys like them make guys like me unappealing to girls like . . . well, girls in general, by calling us faggots, and then when we can't get a date, they think it proves them right."

He looked so angry, I reached over and put my hand on his knee. My chest constricted, and I debated the words I was about to say next, not sure I'd have the courage to say them, but finally I blurted them out.

"We could stop that, you know."

"What?"

"The faggot cycle."

Kenneth glanced over at me.

"How would we do that?"

"Well, if you had a girlfriend . . ."

There was a momentary pause, no longer than a breath, while I waited to see if he would take up my line of thought or pretend he didn't know what I was talking about. There was a universe of potential contained in a bubble of time, and then it burst.

"How would I manage that?" he said. "There aren't exactly girls lining up to date me. That's the whole point."

My heart plummeted into my shoes, and I lifted my hand off his knee. For one moment I was sure my face was completely transparent, but then I slipped my best-friend-Rachel mask back into place.

"All they need to do is *think* you have a girlfriend," I said, keeping my voice extra steady.

"You mean we'd put on a show?"

I shrugged casually, as if this were what I'd meant from the start.

"It wouldn't take much," I said, overcompensating with an airy tone. "A little bit of hand holding. Passing some notes. Telling the right people . . ." I hurried to finish. "You've got to admit it would be a relief, wouldn't it? Not to be in tenth grade and never have had a date?"

There was a long pause.

"Yeah," he admitted at last, "it would be." He looked at me closely. "You'd do that? Pretend, I mean . . ."

I looked at his deep-set eyes and I wanted to say,

I wouldn't have to pretend, but I didn't.

"Yeah, of course. That's what friends are for, right?"

That afternoon, we walked through the hallways hand-in-hand. Bart Sanders saw us and for once he didn't say a word to Kenneth before class, but on Monday when I was on my way to my locker, I saw the familiar crowd of guys outside the science room.

"Butt nugget," I heard someone say.

That's when I knew. No matter how hard we tried, there was no escaping until we'd lived through 535 more days of high school.

Sarah

On a Thursday afternoon during my junior year, I came home from school to find my mother sobbing at the kitchen table.

"Mom, what is it?" I asked, abandoning my backpack and sliding in next to her. She crumpled up the wad of Kleenex in her hand.

"Nothing."

"It's got to be something," I said. "You're crying."

Mom sighed.

"It's your sister," she said. "She's dropping out of school."

"Sarah's dropping out of college?"

Mom nodded.

"I've tried talking to her, but she won't listen. It's bad enough she chose a school all the way across the country, but at least she was *in* school. Any school. Do you know how hard it is to get by without a college degree nowadays?"

I did, because Mom and Dad had told me a million times.

"I just want what's best for her," Mom said, "but she acts like we're her enemies. I don't understand how we could go from being so close to . . ."

Mom stopped talking and blew her nose hard.

"It's that guy she's been dating, isn't it?" Mom said, not a question but a statement. "It's been what? Off and on for over a year now, hasn't it? She must think we're fools if she honestly believes we don't know after all this time."

A laugh escaped Mom's lips, short and bitter.

"I've known since she graduated. Your child doesn't go from spending all of her time in your home to spending eighteen out of every twenty-four hours with 'friends' unless she's in a relationship. I'd just hoped it would end before, well . . . this." She paused, then looked at me. "What's his name, anyway?"

For a moment I considered keeping up Sarah's charade, but then I sighed.

"Jared. Or Jake. Something like that." I paused. "I haven't met him."

Mom nodded, tired. "I told her she could move back home and pay rent, but she says she's moving in with him out in California. I'd give her an ultimatum, but I know what her answer would be."

I nodded, because I knew too and it stung.

Mom fingered the tissue in her hand.

"I just don't understand why having a boyfriend is so much more important than her entire future," she said. "More important than her family . . ."

Her sister.

"I don't know," I answered honestly.

Mom reached out and took my hand.

"I'm glad you're still here," she said, and for a moment Kenneth's theory of graduation flashed through my mind. Would I leave my parents behind when I graduated? Would I leave this town and never look back?

"I'll always be here," I said, and I meant it.

Kenneth

"Don't worry about a thing," Kenneth said, pulling me forward. "They love you already."

I smiled nervously and smoothed out my denim skirt for the hundredth time. I never wore skirts, because they revealed my huge thighs, but today was an exception. Kenneth had invited me to his family reunion, and I wanted to make a good impression.

Together we walked up the long driveway toward his house. It was summer and everyone was on the front lawn. The sound of light jazz and the smell of grilling burgers wafted toward me. A group of kids played volleyball while the adults sat on plastic lawn chairs in semicircles. When we got closer, one circle of adults called out.

"There they are!"

"Oh, he's brought Rachel. . . ."

"Grab another chair."

Kenneth took my hand and led me toward his parents and grandparents.

"Isn't she a sweetheart?" someone whispered.

Kenneth's mother put a hand on my shoulder. "Yes, she is," she said out loud, causing everyone to chuckle. "Such a wonderful girl for our Kenneth. They spend every minute together, you know," she added, winking at Kenneth's father.

I blushed, and beside me Kenneth was blushing too, but he didn't correct them and say that we were just friends, that our boyfriend-girlfriend act was just for school. Instead he said, "Rachel is on student government. She's going to run for senior class president this coming year."

He beamed, but I glared.

"I am not," I said. "We've discussed this. No one would vote for me as class president over Christy Collins."

Kenneth turned quickly.

"That's so not true," he said, seriously. "I know plenty of people who would vote for you, because you'd be great at the job. You've been a class officer for the last two years . . ."

"Secretary," I said, interrupting.

". . . and you've got to remember that popularity in high school isn't about being in the majority. The so-called popular kids are actually the elite minority, while the rest of us make up the base of the pyramid. The popular kids would vote for Christy Collins, but the rest of us would all vote for *you*."

Kenneth's dad offered me a paper plate with a freshly grilled hamburger on it.

"Kenneth is right," he said. "I was class president in high school, and it really is about who will do the best job. The senior class officers need to be responsible and trustworthy, because they'll be in charge of planning all the reunions after you graduate. Very important."

"Do you want our reunions to suck?" Kenneth asked in mock fear.

"I thought you weren't going to any of the reunions," I said, frowning.

"I'd go if you were planning them."

There was a chorus of encouragement, and I could

feel myself warming to the idea. Maybe I *could* be a good class president. I liked being secretary well enough.

Kenneth's dad put his arm around me.

"This little lady can do anything she sets her mind to," he said, giving me a warm squeeze. "We're hoping someday she'll be a part of this—"

The rest of what he said was drowned out by Kenneth's mother's cry of "Daniel, you're embarrassing her!"

I looked over to see Kenneth redder than I had ever seen him. My cheeks were flushed too, but mostly it was my heart that was beating as if I'd just run a marathon.

Later, when things settled down, I pulled him aside.

"Can I talk to you alone for a minute?"

"Sure," he said, setting down his plate of chips and half-eaten burger.

I took his hand and pulled him under the cherry tree in his front yard, slightly away from everyone else. The sky was a crystal clear blue, and a warm breeze wafted past. I leaned my back against the tree trunk, still holding tight to Kenneth's hand. It was the perfect moment I'd been waiting for.

"What's up?" Kenneth asked.

I took a deep breath and launched myself forward, allowing the world to come unglued. I leaned in, closed my eyes, and pressed my lips against his.

Like a flash of light, a memory flickered across my brain before I could stop it. There I was, nine years old, hiding behind the curtains at the edge of the bay window, watching Sarah kiss her first boyfriend in our front yard. I'd so wanted to be her.

And now it was my turn.

I waited for Kenneth's lips to part, for him to wrap his arms around me, his hands snaking across my back. I waited for the warmth of embarrassment to turn into the warmth of passion, but it didn't. Kenneth pulled away gently. The kiss was a truncated peck, sloppy and quick.

When I opened my eyes, he was looking at me, his deep-set eyes apologetic.

"I . . ."

My stomach lurched and I looked down, studying my worn leather sandals against the green of the grass.

"Sorry," I said. "I wanted to do that . . . just once."

The words were rushed and slurred.

Kenneth's face crumpled.

"Rach, it's just . . . I . . . there's something . . ."

I shook my head, my cheeks on fire.

"It's okay," I said. "It was a whim. I don't even know why—"

The words caught in my throat and Kenneth reached out for my hand, but I didn't let him take it.

"Let's go back," I said, walking away, heading toward his family, who waited for us with their knowing smiles. I wanted to stop breathing right then, but I pushed forward, determined not to let the situation get worse than it already was.

But apparently I didn't have a choice.

When we reached the semicircle of lawn chairs, there was someone sitting there I hadn't expected to see.

Sarah.

"Hi," she said, interrupting a conversation she was having to glance up at me. "I've been looking for you."

She held a plate with a watermelon slice on her lap, and everyone was grinning at her as if she were the guest of honor even though she couldn't have been present for more than five minutes.

"What are you doing here?" I stammered, but Sarah just grinned. I could tell that here, in front of this audience, she wanted to play the starring role of my big sister.

"Mom said you were here. Jordan and I are going to a movie, and I thought it might be fun to double date with my little sister and her man."

"We can't," I said. "This is a family reunion. Kenneth and I can't just leave to go to a movie."

"What?" Kenneth's mom said. "You must!"

"Don't get stuck here with us old people!"

The chorus was loud and relentless and my head throbbed. I could feel the world beginning to swirl. I bit my lower lip, wondering if I looked as horrible as I felt.

"It's the new movie with Orlando Bloom," Sarah cajoled. "You know how hot Orlando Bloom is."

Kenneth's hand found the grip it had been seeking before. He squeezed tight.

"Come on, Rachel," he said. "It'll be fun. Please?"

Finally, I nodded. We said our good-byes, then headed to Jordan's pimped-out 2000 Camaro. Later, as

Sarah and I stood in the concession line to get popcorn, she elbowed me in the ribs.

"So, you and Kenneth are turning up the heat," she said with a wink.

I knew right then that she'd seen us under the cherry tree. But what had she seen? How had it looked to her?

For a split second, I wanted to tell her everything. I wanted to lean on her shoulder the way I had when we were small and she'd read me stories with pictures she had drawn herself. I wanted a sister I could confess to, so I could tell her how I'd been such a fool, how stupid I was to sit close to Kenneth on the couch when we'd stay up late watching movies, hoping he'd move in closer; how lame I was to have pretended to be his girlfriend for so long, hoping the imaginary would somehow become real. How could I have been so blind?

"He's cute in a geeky way," Sarah said. "I bet he's really into you."

We were almost to the concession stand. I opened my mouth, a thousand confessions on the tip of my tongue, but nothing came out.

"Thanks," I said, at last. "Jordan's cute too."

Kenneth

I had exactly thirty-two hours to get my graduation speech written, but from the basement, Bob Dylan's "The Times They Are a-Changin'" was blasting up at me and I knew I'd end up writing a big cliché. Wasn't that what everyone did when they had to give a graduation speech?

"There's a time for every season under heaven," I jotted on my notepad. Then I groaned, crumpled up the paper, and threw it at the trash can. Of course I missed. I could be standing directly over my target and somehow my shot would ricochet in the wrong direction. Today it bounced off the rim and hit Kenneth in the crotch as he walked in to my room.

"Thanks for the warm welcome," he said, shutting the door behind him. I couldn't help it. Even though we'd given up our boyfriend-girlfriend act after the family reunion last summer, my heart still fluttered, and for a second I had to look down at my paper, pretending I'd had an important thought. There were days when I was still convinced that everything might change, and

I ached with that thought.

"Sorry," I said, pulling myself together. "You know what a horrible shot I am." I paused. "When did you get here? I never even heard the doorbell."

"Not long ago," Kenneth answered vaguely.

"I probably didn't hear you because of this stupid sixties music Sarah keeps blasting. I swear she does it on purpose to drive me crazy. Ever since she moved home, she acts like she owns the place."

"I like sixties music," Kenneth said, sitting down on my beanbag chair. "Those were revolutionary times. Did you know that the nineteen sixties held more—"

"Not now, Kenneth," I interrupted. "I'm having a crisis. I don't have time for historical trivia. Right now the only history I'm interested in is ours."

"Speech writing?"

"What tipped you off?" I glanced at the pages of notes that now lay scattered in front of my computer.

"Lucky guess."

"The thing is I don't have any words of wisdom to impart. I mean, what the hell have we really learned in the past four years? Algebra? A few words of workable

Spanish? How to survive gym class?"

Kenneth held up one hand in a stop position.

"That's it in a nutshell," he said.

"Gym?"

"No. Survival."

"I don't get it."

"Graduation is a ritual marking the fact that we've survived high school and can now move on to our real lives. Once we graduate, we're adults—in control of our own destinies."

"That's deep, Obi-Wan," I said, but my mind was already beginning to work with his theme. Survival. Is that what high school had been all about? Surviving all the crap so we could get on to bigger and better things?

I jotted down a note and leaned back in my chair.

"So, what are you doing here? I thought you had band rehearsal."

Kenneth shrugged. "I blew it off."

"You did?" I said, narrowing my eyes. "That's not like you."

Kenneth had been doing a lot of things "not like him" in the last month.

"Maybe it is," he said, "and I just never knew it. Perhaps this graduation thing is unlocking a whole new grown-up part of me."

"Really?" I said, incredulous. "You sound like Sarah."

There was a split second when Kenneth's face hardened, shutting me out, but then it changed again. "What's wrong with that?" he said.

"Sounding like Sarah?"

"No. Saying that graduation is making me grow up."

I paused. "I don't know," I said truthfully. "I guess I just have my doubts that one event can change things so significantly. It's not like we cross some line and nothing is ever the same. If that's true, when exactly does everything change? Now, since classes are done and we're just waiting to get our diplomas? Once we shake hands onstage with the principal? The next day when we wake up and lounge around the house for summer vacation?"

"How about college?"

"Maybe," I said, as below us Sarah changed the CD

from Dylan to John Lennon. "But college doesn't work for everyone. Maybe some people never grow up."

"Geez, Rach." Kenneth frowned. "This is going to be one hell of a graduation speech. Can't you just say that graduating is awesome and leave it at that?"

I couldn't tell if he was joking or annoyed.

I turned back to my desk.

"You're right," I said. "I overthink things. Graduation is going to be awesome, no doubt about it."

Kenneth took a deep breath.

"Rach?"

"Yeah?"

There was a long pause.

"I'll miss your overthinking. No matter what happens after graduation, I hope you never change."

"I won't," I said, smiling.

But I was wrong.

Rachel

Graduation morning was cloudless, seventy-eight degrees, with a slight breeze blowing in from the northwest. All the seniors had been instructed to gather outside behind the bleachers at seven forty-five in the morning, dressed in our caps and gowns, tassels to the right.

On the football field, the stage had been set and two hundred white plastic folding chairs dotted the grass. Already most of the spectators were present, milling around the bleachers, looking for the perfect spot to set up their video cameras. Mom and Dad hovered next to me, Mom tugging at my honors sash until it was exactly even.

"I can't believe our baby is graduating high school," Mom said.

I groaned. "Ma . . ."

"I know, I know. But a mother can't help getting sentimental at times like this. My little girl growing up."

Dad rolled his eyes, then gave me a conspiratorial wink.

"I think we'd better get to the bleachers," he said, looking around. "Where did Sarah go?"

Mom sighed. "I'm sure she's found some of her old friends who are home for the occasion. Let's go ahead and get seats. She'll find us when she's ready."

Mom moved to go, but then she turned back and

rushed forward to hug me clumsily. She held on tight for a long while.

"I'm proud of you," she whispered before she let go. "You've turned into a strong young woman."

"Thanks, Ma," I whispered, reaching for her hand, but Dad was already pulling her away toward the bleachers. I stood there following them with my eyes until I couldn't make out their shapes any longer. Mom's words rang in my ears.

A strong young woman. Was I? Simply because I would soon be handed a diploma with my name on it? I didn't feel any different. Excited, nervous, maybe even proud, but not different. Not yet grown up.

I took a deep breath.

Kenneth would say I was dangerously close to overthinking, and he'd made me promise I would not *think* about graduating from high school. I would simply do it and have fun.

Kenneth.

I peered into the crowd, wondering where he could be. I'd called first thing that morning to see if he wanted to drive over together, but he was already gone, probably heading over early for band setup. I'd looked for him in the halls before I went outside as well, but he was strangely absent.

I stopped my friend Marie as she was passing by.

"Have you seen Kenneth?"

She shook her head, then grinned at me. "Finished your speech?"

I nodded, distracted. "If you see him, tell him I'm looking for him."

"Sure thing."

I walked through the throng of seniors, dodging parents and teachers and ignoring Mr. Falhauser, who was madly trying to separate the parents, herding them toward the bleachers with wild gesticulations.

Marvin Blankerman, first trumpet, walked past, and I grabbed his arm.

"Did you guys set up already?"

"Yeah."

"Did you see Kenneth?"

"He's here," Marvin said. "I saw him walking with your sister just a couple minutes ago."

I paused. "Oh."

A hot sensation crept up my spine.

Our principal was now herding the seniors into a vague semblance of the two straight lines we'd been instructed to form during practice. I stood in the middle of the crowd, completely out of sequence, staring blankly.

"Five minutes, people," Mr. Falhauser called, his voice far away.

I tried to focus on breathing.

Sarah. My mind was already fitting together the stray pieces of a puzzle I still didn't want to admit existed.

For more than a month now, Kenneth had been giddy and philosophical, busy and annoyingly superior, as if he'd surpassed me in some way. He treated me like an old friend, with a note of pity underlying much of what he said. I'd thought it was a precursor to graduation, distancing himself before the deed was done, but now my heart thumped so hard, I feared I'd need the ambulance the school always parked near the football field for fainters and vomiters.

I moved my feet forward mechanically, making my way down the length of both lines, straining my neck to see over the crowd, oblivious to Mr. Falhauser's calls of

"Three minutes now!"

Then, like the moment of revelation in a mystery movie, I knew where I would find them. They'd be at the spot where everyone went to kiss the loves of their lives before a big high school event. It was the spot where the football players kissed the cheerleaders and the kids on the track team made out before a meet. It was supposed to be hidden from view, but if I took three more steps . . .

I knew beyond a shadow of a doubt that I should not move.

But, of course, I did.

I shuffled toward the bleachers until I could see them there, leaning against the metal framework of the stands. Several other couples dotted the shady landscape. Sarah was pressing against him, her hips lined up with his, her long hair loose down her back.

I watched as they parted and she took out her favorite cherry-flavored lip gloss and applied it seductively. It was a move I'd seen her use on a hundred boys before, and for a split second I knew that she saw me, that as she smudged her lips together, she was looking straight at me. Daring me to grow up.

Then she and Kenneth disengaged and Mr. Falhauser caught my elbow and ushered me toward my place in line.

"Let's go, Rachel," he said. "We need you up front. You've got an important speech to give. Can't be late."

My speech.

As I followed his lead, my mind was utterly blank. Everything I'd ever known had vanished, replaced instead with nothing.

I looked at the papers that I was unwittingly crumpling in my balled-up grip, the first line of my speech staring up at me: *After four long years we have finally made it.* I closed my eyes, then wadded up the pages and threw them at the nearest garbage can. For once, a perfect shot.

"What are you doing?" Tara Miller, class secretary, asked. "Wasn't that your speech?"

I nodded.

"Well, do you have it memorized?"

I laughed, a short, bitter laugh. "Far from it."

But though I no longer knew the words, I knew what

I was going to say. A single word flashed across my brain and would not leave.

Survival.

Now I understood. This wasn't what we learned from high school; it was what we learned from life. It was what we would *always* have to learn again and again. No invisible line would be crossed, no diploma handed out, no age limit surpassed that would ever change this fact.

I took a deep breath.

From somewhere behind us, Mr. Falhauser's voice rang out.

"Seniors, proceed."

Our procession was ushered onto the football field, one by one, each of us crossing over. The crowd rose, their applause constant, deafening. Each holler and whistle, every metallic stomp magnified. At first my feet stumbled, heavy and awkward, my palms sweaty, my breath short, but then I looked at the stage, empty and vast, waiting for me.

I took one step forward, then another, moving on.

Joanna Breitstein

K. L. Going is an award-winning author of books for children and teens. Her first novel, *Fat Kid Rules the World*, was named a Michael Printz Honor Book by the American Library Association as well as one of the Best Books for Young Adults from the past decade. She has also written *The Liberation of Gabriel King*, *Saint Iggy*, and *Garden of Eve*. Her books have been BookSense picks, Scholastic Book Club choices, Junior Library Guild selections, and winners of state book awards, and have been featured by *Publishers Weekly*, *School Library Journal*, and the Children's Book Council as best books. K. L. began her career working at one of the oldest literary agencies in New York City. She currently lives in Glen Spey, New York, where she both writes and runs a business critiquing manuscripts. You can visit her online at www.klgoing.com.

The Longest Distance

Beth Kephart

Even when you don't ask, you have asked by the way you look at me—by how you try to hold my eye, try to suggest (a touching gesture) that it is concern you feel, not curiosity. But if I had answers, don't you think that I'd confess them? That I'd have said by now, put out a proclamation, that Joelle died for this, or for that. That she died *because.* All I can tell you is what you know, which is: Joelle is gone. She's the slash of black you see just after lightning breaks the sky. She's the place where a cliff stops being stone and becomes the air that you could fall through.

I was her best friend, only and always. Now she exists in my mind. I carry thoughts of her everywhere I go. I scrunch up my eyes so that I don't lose sight of all that she might have been.

*

Mom says, "Honey?" with a question mark, and that's her *How are you doing?* That's her thinking that she's not crowding me all around with questions, that she's giving me equal parts love and room. She got into the habit right after it happened, and in our house habits are glue. Once we start doing one thing, we don't trade it for another. Habits make living easy, Dad says. Habits make it possible. This is what he says when he's headed out the door.

I set the alarm for six each day.

I hit the five-minute snooze.

I brush my teeth before I eat to get out the taste of last night. I eat and brush again. I pull on my clothes and I run for the bus and nobody ever sits beside me. The seat beside me is the seat that Joelle filled. First grade through March third a year and two months ago.

It was a Saturday morning when I found out. It was my mom who came to tell me. I had heard the ringing of the phone through a dream. I heard a sudden something, a rustling, sounds that were getting in my way. "Hannah?" my mother said, and she was sitting right there on my Mexican quilt, pulling the colors tight across me, making it hard for me to breathe, and there was something she had to say but couldn't, and I knew right then that a huge big bad unfixable had happened. There was the dirty rub of yesterday's mascara beneath my mother's eyes, wetness on her cheeks. There was a catch in her voice, the way that she started and stopped and tried to start again.

"Baby," she said, and it was the last time she called me that, it was the last time that anyone would ever, ever think of me as just a girl, as a child-daughter, as Robbie's little sister. My mother lifted my head with the cradle of her hands. She kissed me on the forehead. "It's Joelle," she said, and I said, "No, it isn't." Because I knew that whatever had gone wrong had to be shouted back first, had to be shoved straight out of understanding, if I was going to survive.

"Hannah," she said. "I am so sorry." And now there were rivers flowing from my mother's eyes and down her shape-of-Pennsylvania cheeks and disappearing past her U-turn chin, and I was crying, too, for all that I didn't yet know but soon would have to. For all that I couldn't change about whatever it was that had started the phone ringing in the first place.

How can a best friend—anybody's best friend—go as far away as Joelle? How had I not seen her disappearance coming? I was her best friend. *Best* friend. I was the one who was supposed to know her every single thought. She was the queen of the motes she said—not like castle moat, but like dust-speck motes, those bits that hang suspenseful and still in cones of window light. In autumn, especially, with the sun slanting in just right, I would find her sitting yoga style on the rug of her bedroom floor inside a beam of sun. She'd be holding her hands as if she were catching flakes of snow, naming the colors, the shapes, the qualities of what was floating by. "They're purple, Hannah, can you see them?" she'd ask, and I'd sit beside her and stare like she was staring until I could see the tiny bits, too, which never really rose nor fell. "Afterlife-quality peace," Joelle would say, sad but not mad, the way she said things, and I'd say, "What would you know about the afterlife?" She'd point to the side of her head and say, "Stricken at birth by a cruel imagination."

Which she had been, no doubting that; it was her heritage. It was the primary thing that had put the long stitch down the center of her forehead to just above her nose—her too-young-to-be-so-old line, is what she sometimes called it. Imagination was in her genes, her genius for it going back, on her father's side, to the great-great-great generation. A poet, an inventor, an architect all the way down to Joelle's father, who specialized in risk. There were stories about him in the financial magazines and the *Wall Street Journal*, and even if he was, as Joelle liked to say (emphasizing the underemphasis), a *smidgeon* on the eccentric side, he was trusted for his opinion. He would hole himself up in his office for weeks and then emerge with some solution to some given problem, his eyes big, Joelle said, as cartoon-character eyes, his face white as a baby's tooth. "One half step away from the looney bin," she'd say about him, but she was fine with it, I thought, fine with being his spitting image, fine with all that imagination genius streaming through her blood. She was fine with sad, I thought—a truly serious person, a big thinker, following along in the footsteps of fate. She wasn't full of giggles, didn't have a silly side. She wasn't girly. She had all sides of most equations in her head at the same time, but still she made me believe, made it seem that if only you waited a while longer, you'd emerge on the right side of change. Odds, she always said, had to be with you. Joelle was a brand-new version of ancient wisdom, but she said she felt right-aged with me.

"Tell me your secrets," she would say to me, and I'd think hard until I remembered one I hadn't already shared before—something about a turtle I'd found when I was a girl, something about a bracelet I once stole from a neighbor's jewelry box; I had it still.

Once I said, "I bought you some motes for your birthday," and just like that the seam down Joelle's forehead vanished and her cheeks flushed pink and the sadness lifted long enough for her whole self to break open with laughter. It was the sweetest, rarest, most lovely sound, and when it happened, when laughter triumphed for that one fantastic moment over sad, we fell back, both of us, through the cones of sun.

"You know what genius is?" she asked afterward, lying faceup on her floor.

"What?"

"Genius is finding the funny."

"No way," I said. "Genius is you."

"Genius is the motes," she said. "How they hold themselves up in the spaces in between." She touched her finger to the side of her head and blew a kiss through the room. She sighed long and hard, and I lay there, too, until it got dark and time for home and my own family.

Nobody sits on the bus beside me anymore. For a year and two months I've come and gone in the hollow nothing of Joelle not laughing.

✱

For my senior thesis I'm doing a report on time. My working title is "Time: The Great Houdini Healer," even though it absolutely is not, and I'm writing toward twenty-five pages instead of fifteen, working with eighteen references instead of ten, and when my parents say to come down to dinner, I say I can't, I have this project due, I am in the middle of research, I am in the middle of a sentence, I am in the middle. They're used to this now, but it took them a while. My Dad calls "Dinner!"—brusque, the way he does—and I call "Busy!" harshly back, and a few minutes later my mom will be at my door, a dish in her hand. My mom is a nurse, and she's good with all the food groups. It's ham with green beans and whole-grain rice, or trout with purple potatoes and broccoli, or salad with soup and a heel of bread. They always save me the heel of bread, because I like the challenge, the way the tough crust finally gives in. Even when Robbie still lived here, before he left for the big-time Ivy League, I got both ends of the loaf.

I don't rush my dinner. I chew and chew and chew, and after I'm done, I lie faceup on my bed and contemplate my next sentence, my next category, the things Mr. LaMotte, my thesis advisor, calls segues. I've already got chunks on the solar system—the sun, the moon, the stars. I've got an okay couple of pages on the Sumerians and their thirty-day months, the Egyptians and their moon cycles, the Aztecs and their stones. I learned about obelisks and I put that in. I've got stuff on medieval clocks, on the swinging of Galileo's pendulum, on the ways that atomic clocks are better than quartz ones— even though, to be honest, I don't really know what a lot of that means, can't get my head around terms like *piezoelectric property*, or *cesium*, or *resonance*. I look them up, but it doesn't help. I try to bring them into my mind, "activate" them, like Mr. LaMotte says. I even look at the diagrams, but I've never been stellar with labeled pictures; they're like a language I can't read. So I lie on my bed and I think about next. Next sentence, next topic, next minute, next hour. Next day without Joelle. Next steps. I graduate in twenty-two days. Come next September, someone else will take my place in the old school bus, which means that someone else will take Joelle's, and when that happens, what happens? Will Joelle be gone for good?

Where do ghosts go? What do you do with all the impossible possibilities? How do you find your way through, to the other side of change?

My mother says that I'm working too hard, but you have to work hard if you want to stop time. I want to dial time backward. I want time to heal me. I want to hold myself steady in the spaces in between. If I were to tell my father this, he'd shake his head. My father lives in the realm of the rational.

*

The two girls who sit in front of me on the bus are Annie and Marne. Joelle always called them the fairytale girls, because of their names but also because of their looks— long, blond hair, both of them, Annie with hazel eyes, Marne with brown. Annie is the prettier one. Marne tries hard to keep up. They switch off sweaters, from what I can tell. Belts. They wear the same kind of lip gloss. There are the very best of best friends.

Joelle and I were never like that. We always made our own decisions. We didn't borrow each other's ideas. We talked about everything—I swear we did—but we drew our own conclusions. "You girls are old before your time," Joelle's mom would say, and I would laugh, but Joelle would shrug, and whenever people told me that Joelle was always sad, I would say, But she's smarter than a pile of encyclopedias, smarter than the whole debate team put together, as smart as my own freak brother, Robbie. There is a kind of sad that is genius sad, and that's the way I saw it.

Annie and Marne may be laughing behind their hands, but their laughs are little kaput laughs, over before they get started. They're practically flirty with each other, silly, the *oh-my-god!* kind of girls, and they were always like that—on the bus, in the cafeteria, at football games—always making a show of themselves, like they were posing for reality TV. Except they weren't like that the day I climbed back on the bus, a week after Joelle disappeared. They just stared at me then, with their hazel and brown eyes. "Hannah," they said, both of them turned around, both of them staring open-mouthed at me. "Why did she do it?"

"Because she did," is what I said. And closed my arms across my chest and stared out the window. All the regular things in the neighborhood went by. They looked blurry to me, underwater. I've worn sunglasses to school every day ever since. No one needs to know how I am feeling.

Here are some of the things that have been said about time: "Time brings all things to pass" (Aeschylus). "Time flies over us, but leaves its shadow behind" (Nathaniel Hawthorne). "Time is the longest distance between two places" (Tennessee Williams). "Time, which changes people, does not alter the image we have retained of them" (Marcel Proust).

I collect these things for my senior thesis—go through quote books, copy them down, try to make some sense of them. If Joelle were here, she would give me her opinion, she would study the words with that line down her brow, she would say, "Well, you know . . ." Then she would peel the polish from her fingernail, bite away at it until the shiny shell came free in a single piece. She would not say another word until she was sure of what she thought. She'd sit in her dark blue room, the motes invisible around her, her long legs up on her desk while I lay on the little braided rug on the floor below her—her grandmother's rug, her heirloom rug. Eventually she'd offer something smart that no one else would ever think to say—tell me the story, again, about the longest she ever went without having a thought, tell me the sound that wings make when they're flying back home, tell me about how no one yet had invented a cure for the excessive-imagination gene. Then she'd reach for the bottle of black nail polish and polish up the naked nail.

"You're such an original," I'd tell her.

"Yeah," she'd say, "but what good does that do me? Where does original get you?" She would look out toward the window, the winter sky. She'd get this complicated look inside her dark eyes, and I would lie there, waiting.

But now Joelle was not here, and I didn't know her thoughts; I didn't have any way of asking, and even when I scrunched up my eyes, I couldn't hear what maybe she would say. It was a cocktail of cleaners that killed her, if you have to know, because always the question after Why? is How? Always it's there, the Annie-and-Marne question—and don't think I wasn't mad, don't think that there wasn't anger spewing out along with my oceans and oceans of tears when my mother, sitting on my bed beside me, tried her best to explain. My mother said, "Hannah, I'm so sorry. Hannah. She was alone when it happened; her parents weren't home."

"Alone?" I said. "She was never alone. She had me. She had me. She had *me*." I threw back the colors of the Mexican quilt, and I pushed my mother aside and I went running down the stairs in my red-and-white nightgown, and running down the street, running all five blocks, my mother calling out behind me, my hand at last pounding at the door of Joelle's house. "Joelle!" I shouted, "Joelle, let me in!" and they let me in, they let me in and hugged me hard, but they would not let me see her.

"Remember her as she was," they said.

"As she *was*?" I said, I screamed.

✳

My brother, Robbie, is my family's superstar. He was born special and he stayed special, and it was like he didn't have to try: Success walked right up to him, stuck around, was his never-going-to-leave-him friend. Robbie never even looked goofy, like smart guys are supposed to, and to top it off he was Mr. Sporting Life—tennis, fencing, crew, the sports that rich people are supposed to play, except that we were never rich people. My dad's the accountant for the local newspaper, and my mom only works part-time. We always said Robbie was the family accident, a freak among normals, and he was so smart and so very super special that I didn't mind, I honestly didn't mind, because proximity made me famous. Between having Robbie for a brother and Joelle for a best friend, I kind of slid through school, got a truckload of benefits of the doubt. When I was stuck on something, people assumed that it was temporary, that I was smart enough to figure it out and was having a weird mental block. When I didn't know an answer, teachers slid it my way. When the time came to decide who was A.P. material and who was just plain honors, every teacher of every class promoted me up to A.P., where Joelle was, where Robbie had been. I worked my butt off to maintain my ranking, and it was never, ever easy. You're around smart, you're supposed to be smart. Those are the rules of the game.

Mr. LaMotte says I should make things simpler for myself. That a senior thesis is not a whole big book with a leather cover, but some sheets of paper with a staple. He says that fifteen pages will do. "Really, Hannah," he says, "don't push so hard. Really, you've proven yourself." But I have only three weeks to figure out time, to figure out life. Time was one thing, and now it's something else. The afterlife was just an idea. And now it's a fact, or it isn't.

*

Robbie had a lot of options. He went with Yale. He got up there and he looked around and he said, "This feels like home," although, let me tell you, our house, our little last-house-before-the-cul-de-sac house, bears no resemblance to Yale or to any of the other millions of colleges we visited for Robbie's sake, my parents taking me along on every trip, a two-for-oner is what they said. Yale is lots of green walled in by stone. Yale is permanent, and old. It's like a whole little city inside another city, and it didn't take much to picture Robbie there, in the center of the center. Robbie's genius is the uncomplicated kind. He lets it lead him around by the nose.

Me? I'm just glad I went on Robbie's college-seeing trips. I'm just glad we did all that ahead of Joelle's being gone. Because I didn't want to go anywhere after that; I didn't want to move, and when it came time for college applications, it was my dad, my super-rational dad, who got me through it. Every night at the kitchen table, for a month or two, he sat reading to me from the college books, showing me more on his laptop, talking me through the pros and cons of big college versus small college, urban college versus rural college, east coast versus west coast. We even looked at Scotland until my mother called, from the other room, "Honey? Isn't Scotland a whole ocean away?" My dad, being an accountant, has patience for this. He kept spooling through the choices until something sounded good. "Let's think about your opportunities," he'd say, and *opportunities* was a good word, was a whole lot less scary than *choices*. "If you get there and find it doesn't fit," he'd say, "there's always the transfer option."

I decided that I wanted small. I decided that I wanted suburban but close to a city. I decided that I wanted to take classes that could help me think my way more accurately through life, because really and truly, even though Dad didn't say it, even though I was still thinking tons about what Joelle could have been, where we might have gone together, I got that I was on my own. I wouldn't have Joelle to count on. I had to count on me. I'd visited Haverford College with Robbie. I decided, with my dad's help, to make that my number-one choice. Afterward I worked, with Dad, on the applications—for Haverford, for the backups. It was what we did when Mom cleaned up the kitchen, or sat at her little desk in the family room answering her emails, or watched what she called her guilty-pleasure TV, that stupid bachelor show. My dad and I worked all last fall. We were getting somewhere, together. And then I started my senior thesis, and I was on my own. "Leave her be," I heard my dad tell my mom one night. "She's got a lot of sorting to do."

*

"Time heals what reason cannot." That's what Seneca says, and I hate, hate, hate that I never ever got the chance to hear Joelle on Seneca, that it never even occurred to me that she'd be gone before I had her opinion, that she would, in the end, stop believing in the the change she'd always promised me was coming. I knew that she was sad, but who was I to criticize the thoughts of a serious person? How was I to know that she'd grown any sadder than before? She had been talking about purpose, toward the end. She had been saying that it was a difficult concept. She had been listing all the things that people do that add straight up to nothing. Annie and Marne, the fairytale girls: What was *their* purpose? she asked me. What about the woman next door, who never came out of her house except to walk her Jack Russell terrier over to the birch tree? What about politicians, who go speechifying all day but can't find a way to make things better? What about the meter maid, who walks around town, penalizing people for lateness?

"My grandmother," Joelle said, "made rugs. She made so many rugs that she practically went blind, and why? What was the purpose of the rugs? People *walk* on rugs."

"Maybe she just liked to make rugs," I said, but Joelle would have none of it. It wasn't that Joelle argued back, because she never did, at least with me. She just chose not to agree. Were those warning signs? Would you call them that? Would you have done something different, had you been me? Should I have called someone up? Told a parent? Scheduled a meeting with Mr. LaMotte? Had I been looking at something that I couldn't see? I was her best friend. Her *best* friend. I blame myself for not listening well enough. For not noticing that she was through with waiting.

Time heals what reason cannot.

Come on, Houdini. Heal me.

You could write about time forever and ever and miss out on some of the key facts. You could write in circles. I was mostly almost done with my senior thesis when

I came across stuff on water clocks and decided that I had to fit that in. Water clocks were like hourglasses, but without the sand—they were bowls made out of stone, the bottoms punched with a tiny hole. Through the hole the water dripped, while etched-out lines on the bowls' insides marked how the time was passing. Time was a drip, drip, drip. An Egyptian pharaoh had a water clock in his tomb, and the Greeks liked the idea of them too. The Greeks even had a word for them, a word I understand, *clepsydras*, which means water thieves. Water thieves. I think that's just perfect. Joelle, I'm almost sure of this, would have loved the concept, too, put it right up there high, with her afterlife of motes. I do my research on water thieves and write it up, for both of us. I scrunch my eyes and I can almost see Joelle saying, sighing, "Well, you know."

Then I lie down on my bed and I close my eyes and I dream of water clocks. I dream of the Egyptians and of the Greeks and of the Chinese, and water in bowls, and water over wheels and water in an endless drip, and when I wake, there is a storm outside. I can hear the rain falling down on the roof, the rain collecting in the gutters that go across the house and then down the house, spilling into my mother's white azalea garden. There are little gurgles of thunder but no white strikes. There are times when the rain comes hard, then eases off, like someone leaning against the window, then moving away, then coming back again, craving attention. Where does a soul go after a body's gone? Maybe it comes down at you in raindrops.

"Joelle." I say her name out loud, and all of a sudden I remember another rainy day, two summers before, just after Joelle got her license. "We're going to the beach," she told me that day, and it was just a boring old Tuesday and Joelle had a secondhand car, and our parents approved, so we went—Joelle picking me up from my house around ten o'clock, her towel and her beach bag in the Honda's backseat. She had her aviator shades on, her hair up in a knot, a map thrown down on the passenger's side. "You're navigating," she said when I got in, but of course she didn't need any help from me; she always knew where she was going. I sat back and I let her drive. The windows of the car were down. The wind messed with our hair.

It was a ninety-minute drive, maybe, and when we'd started there was sun with clouds, but as we got closer, it was mostly clouds, some sun. I was watching the sky, and Joelle was, too, but the darkening of the day did not concern her. The closer we got, the slower she drove. "Do you hear the gulls?" she asked, and I said, "Yes." "Do you smell the seaweed?" she wanted to know, and I guessed that I did (except what is a seaweed smell?) and nodded. She had a black T-shirt on and baggy pants, a tank suit under that. She had never turned the music on. We mostly drove in silence, Joelle concentrating, because she'd never driven so far before. We'd never gone off to the beach by ourselves, gone off like this, together.

"Do you know what I like?" she asked, when we were blocks from the shore, when her grip on the steering wheel got lighter.

I shook my head no, didn't want to look stupid with a bad guess.

"I like the way the ocean seems to go on and on forever."

I waited.

"I mean, think about it, Hannah."

"Yeah?"

"The ocean is ocean way past the horizon."

I nodded.

"It's probably even deeper than sky."

"Uh-huh."

"The ocean doesn't have to think, because it just is. Imagine just being, not thinking."

We drove by the ice-cream shop, the rafts-and-buckets store, the fudge-and-taffy vendor. We drove by people in flip-flops and sunblock, drove slow. There was this little kid dragging this big, huge garden shovel, and Joelle took her eyes from the road, just for a second, to watch him. "All the way to China," she said, and now we were right up as close as a car could get to that particular shore. She pulled into a parking spot, shook her hands free of the old steering wheel. "That was easier than I thought it'd be," she said, and I laughed and she shrugged; then we reached into the backseat for our stuff. We walked the hot sidewalk to the planked boardwalk, between the sea grasses and the dunes. We walked across the sand that went from soft and hot to hard and cool.

The clouds kept coming in more thickly, and the tide was out. There was plenty of room on that beach for us. Joelle chose a spot and we flopped out our beach towels—put them side by side to make an almost square and sat down to face the waves. We were close enough to the water's edge to see the little pinkish-shelled clams coming up for air before digging back in. There were gulls beaking around for scraps, checking out a washed-up horseshoe crab, tiptoeing around the squirmy bits of jellyfish. An older couple walked slowly by, her leaning into him. Four girls in white bikinis. A couple of guys. Behind us were the others who did not mind the clouds, and there was a game of volleyball a little farther down, a game of tag. There was that kid with his shovel, digging in, his father sitting beside him in a striped canvas chair, reading a newspaper. Joelle was my best friend. I knew to let her be. To wait for her to talk, or to sit there silently.

"You think it will rain?"

I looked up. The clouds were thick. "Maybe," I said.

"Well, you know," she said.

I waited.

"Rain could be pretty cool." She seemed happy with the idea of it. I was happy because she was.

The day went by, and we sat. The kid behind us dug deeper. The tide had turned, the water was coming back in, and little by little there were fewer people out on the beach, holes in the sand where the sun umbrellas had been, no more volleyball, and somehow or other, I couldn't guess how, the older couple had made it across the hard sand to the soft sand to the asphalt beyond. I had my own opinion about what should happen next, but Joelle had driven and that meant she was in charge, and I pulled an extra towel over my shoulders, because of the breeze that had started to blow, more like a wind. The ocean had gone from green blue to green gray—big waves way out there, curls of white toward the shore, a line of sea foam at the very edge, the little clams in their pastel-colored shells not coming up for air anymore, the horseshoe crab grabbed back by the tide.

I felt the first drop of rain in the side part of my hair. I felt the second on the knuckle of the ring finger of my right hand. Soon the ocean had bigger waves and the pucker marks of rain. It was the sound of something coming toward us. All around us people were gathering up their things. They were running toward the soft sand and the planked walk so that they might beat the storm.

But Joelle—she still had her wide shades on. She wasn't taking cover. She stood. She stretched her arms out straight. She turned, a perfect circle, her face thrown back to catch the rain.

"This is so incredibly perfect," she said.

"What are you going to do?" I asked.

"Take a swim," she said. "Of course."

She didn't take her glasses off, or her T-shirt, her baggy pants. She didn't turn back, toward me. She just kept on walking, through the rain, across the foam, toward the waves, up to her shoulders. She started bobbing then, keeping her face above the line of water, until she lay straight back and floated, and sometimes the waves got high and I couldn't see her, and then they settled and there she was—her long legs, her long, wet ponytail, her eyes behind her shades. She was, she always was, so original.

The rain by now was coming on strong. My towel was

getting wetter, my hair streaking through. I wrapped my arms around my legs, rested my chin on my knees, shivered and tried to stop myself from shivering. But I didn't call her back. I wouldn't call her back. I just watched her ride the storm. She splashed and went still. She splashed and went still. I could almost see her smiling. Even the boy with the shovel had left his dig. Except for a dog down the way, we were alone. The sky was all clouds and the sea was all gray, and then something spectacular happened. Something I remember now, this night, just twenty-two days before I graduate, after I dream of stone bowls keeping track of time, dream of the Egyptians and the Greeks. Out past Joelle in that storm, in that sea, came a gorgeous slice of silver. It rose, it fell, it rose again, and within it she, the queen of the motes, was perfectly suspended. It took me a while before I understood that the dolphins had come to Joelle, that perhaps she had drawn them toward her. She waited for something, I'll never know what, then reached out with her long arms to touch them. Then it was the most complete stillness, like nothing moved at all—not the dolphins, not Joelle, not the sea. Nothing rising, nothing falling, the slightest hint of purple.

"The ocean just is," Joelle had said, and right then Joelle just was, too. It wasn't purpose that she wanted in that one moment, but living, which is better. It wasn't questions, but answers. She was alive in the sea and the storm. She was alive; she was happy; she was calm. *This is so incredibly perfect.* And this is the image that I wake with this night—Joelle in the company of dolphins, Joelle in balance. Down on the roof, into the gutters, into my mother's garden, the rain is falling, and suddenly I am crying. "Mom?" I call, and she calls, "Honey?" and she is here, in my room, on my bed, on my quilt, cradling my head in her hands. She is here, and that is all I need. I don't say anything, and Mom doesn't ask me.

"I think I finished my senior thesis." Finally, I tell her.

"Oh, honey," she says. "I'm so glad."

*

The next morning my dad says, "Can I drive you to school?" and I say that I would like that. And he waits for me, he reads his paper, while I have my breakfast and brush my teeth a second time, and print out my thesis, hammer a single staple through it. He's not rushing out the door, which isn't entirely rational.

"You've done a lot of work," he says, and I nod.

"I'd love to read it," he tells me, "when you're ready."

I say that maybe I'll be ready soon, and he puts his arm across my shoulders as we make our way out onto the drive. He walks me to the passenger's side, opens my door, waits for me to climb inside, closes me in. The streets are wet from the night before. There's a silver glisten on the leaves of trees, on the lips of irises and tulips, on other people's cars, on the porch of Mr. Watkins's house next door, which is still wrapped up with Christmas lights despite the fact that it is May. We drive past everything familiar, everything I'll leave when this summer ends and I'm packed for Haverford. I wonder how this place will look in memory, when I think about it later.

"Hannah?" Dad says, and I turn toward him, study him—his really large and really great green eyes.

"Yeah, Dad?"

"What do you say we drop your thesis off to Mr. LaMotte, then take a drive somewhere?" He scratches the side of his head the way he does when he feels shy, when he isn't really certain about an answer, which is hardly ever at all. People are people, my dad once said. It's numbers that follow the rules.

"Don't you have to go to work?" I ask.

"What's one day?" he says. "Who's going to miss me?"

But I know that everyone at his work will miss him, because they all depend on Dad. I know that he hasn't gone off for an unscheduled day for years, that he goes to work no matter what, that if he has any pride at all, it's a pride that is all wrapped up with his not actually nerdy but weirdly indestructible reliability. "You mean it?" I ask.

"Of course I mean it," he answers. "You finished your thesis. We should go and celebrate."

"All right," I say, trying to imagine where we might go, how far one can travel in one day. *Time is the longest distance between two places.* Thank you, Tennessee Williams.

"All right?" Dad stops scratching his head, takes a long look at me. "Did you say all right?"

"Yeah," I say. "All right. Absolutely." I shrug my shoulders, up and down. And then, in spite of myself, I laugh, and when I stop, the world's not quite as hollow.

W. Sulit

Beth Kephart is the author of the National Book Award finalist *A Slant of Sun: One Child's Courage*. She also wrote the teen novels *Nothing but Ghosts, House of Dance*, and *Undercover*, as well as *Into the Tangle of Friendship: A Memoir of Things that Matter; Still Love in Strange Places: A Memoir; Seeing Past Z: Nurturing the Imagination in a Fast-Forward World; Ghosts in the Garden; Endings, Beginnings, and the Unearthing of Self; Zenobia: The Curious Book of Business;* and *Flow: The Life and Times of Philadelphia's Schuylkill River*. Beth won both the Speakeasy Poetry Prize and a Pew Fellowship in the Arts in 2005. She is a ballroom dancer and an avid gardener in Pennsylvania, where she lives with her family. You can visit her online at www.beth-kepart.blogspot.com.

Arrangements

Chris Lynch

 The thing to remember about a funeral is that it's not about you. At least you hope it's not.

My dad, Charlie Waters Sr., five feet six, weighed 310 pounds when he died. Thank goodness for the cancer boiling him down at the end there. Can you imagine what it would have cost to buy a suit, size Godzilla short, that was only ever going to be worn once anyway? It would have been the suit or the coffin, but there was no budget for both.

Dad would have understood that. He didn't under-stand the small but significant things, like *Butter by itself is not a snack*. But he understood big stuff, such as *It's not about you*. Possibly more than anyone ever, Charlie Waters Sr. understood it's not about you.

Which is why, in an odd way, he wound up in the

pawnbroker business. He understood it was about every-body else. Which was why he was an uncommonly unsuccessful and well-loved pawnbroker.

Which is why I, Charlie Waters Jr., age nineteen, am now in the pawnbroker business.

And I have a burden: My dad was a nice guy in a very unnice business. Senior's business is now Junior's business.

Dad insisted—*insisted*—on appearing at his own wake with a big smile across his face. Whatever the process is in the funeral business for freezing a toothy smile on a guy—probably involving toothpicks, since the undertaker was a local—they must have undertaken it, because Dad lit up the proceedings with this electro grin like the expression on a very fat skeleton head. Some people found the effect unsettling.

I just kept thinking, *What are you smiling at?* Even when I caught the urge to smile along with him.

The funeral saw nearly everybody in the town in attendance, because Charlie Waters Sr. was basically the guv'nor of the place. When the guv'nor of a place is the broker of pawns, that place is an unfortunate place.

Lundy Lee is that place. It sits at the tip of a peninsula that sticks out like a finger pointing to all the places across the sea that you would really rather go. The closest thing to the tip of that finger is the Big Island, which is really not big by any standards other than those of Lundy Lee.

There is a ferry port in the town, and that is the main thing. The way a big nice clock would bong in a nice town, the ferry bops a couple times a day between the Lee and the Big Island, and then on to someplace else that nobody is quite sure about because nobody has ever gone away on it and bothered to come back and tell the rest of us.

Mrs. Waters, wife of Charlie, mother of Charlie, was one of those. Took that cruise to nowhere but somehow forgot that nowhere was a round trip. She'll remember eventually, though. That's one of the few things Dad and I seriously disagreed on. I figure people always come back. Until they don't. My mother hasn't not come back yet.

So Dad's funeral was filled with the people of the town, as well as most of the people who had disembarked from the eleven-fifteen ferry, because that's how it is when you disembark from a ferry. You follow along with everybody else, obeying the flow of traffic and peer pressure, and since the funeral was the absolute only activity in Lundy Lee that day, what with the ferry being already in and the pawn shop being closed, that meant everybody came to a stop at the funeral of the guv'nor.

One hundred and fifteen mourners at the very least. Biggest gathering in the town in years, and all the locals had it marked on their calendars for days—the more observant ones for months if they'd noticed his sickly decline. Even the boat people almost all knew who Charlie was, because Big Islanders not only passed through Lundy Lee a lot, they often made special trips over, to see the sights—there is a cannon on a hill aimed at the Big Island for some reason—and to ask generous, soft-inside-soft-outside Charlie Waters Sr. if he could maybe give them a few too many bucks for the bicycle, flugelhorn, or framed authentic photograph of General Ulysses S. Grant that came straight out of *Life* magazine, but that nobody wanted out on the island.

Every crew member on the boat knew my father.

He cashed dubious checks, advanced payday pay well before payday, taking a stained sailor's hat for collateral. The kitchen guy came in with a foot-long whitefish and cabbage sandwich, asking for a week's advance, and Dad didn't say no.

He never said no to a sandwich. Not even whitefish and cabbage. Jesus, did he stink sometimes, and Jesus, did I love him. The other thing he could never say no to was people. He considered his job to be public service, a calling, and that is what he handed down to his son.

I knew the day was coming. I didn't know for a whole long time, since Dad never went to the doctor and therefore didn't realize he had tumors until he was about equal parts tumor and Charlie, but I did have some time to prepare myself. Not time enough to get a proper running start away from the responsibility and the new, real life I was bequeathed, but time enough to see it coming my way.

I never wanted this. He wanted me to want it, even though he knew I didn't want it.

Now, standing in front of the mesh cage that protects

the plate-glass window that carries the logo, BREAD&WATERS LOANS, in arching burnt-orange letters, as if the sun were always rising on this particular window, Charlie Waters Jr. isn't a happy-happy guy.

I'm not alone, either. The shop has been closed for a week for all the mourning, and so there is to be expected a slight backlog of business this day. My first day.

"Where'd the fat man go?" asks the voice behind me. I can just see the reflection of a face in the window, as if I've sprouted a second, swollen, white head from my shoulder.

"He's gone where all the fat men go," I say, shrugging. The extra head doesn't move.

"McDonald's."

"No, the other place."

"Dead?"

"'Fraid so."

"Who you, then?"

"Fat man Junior."

"You ain't even fat. You got my concertina?"

"I don't know for certain, sir, but I'm guessing I probably do have your concertina."

This is a salty sea dog, following me into the shop for the start of the first day of my new life with my own business and without my own father. Right off the boat, this salty sea dog. Or more likely, judging from his essence, off the boat sometime yesterday, wandering around the bars and benches for twenty-four hours waiting to be reunited with his concertina.

"I got my ticket," says Salty.

I wade in unfamiliar, like I haven't been here hundreds of times before. Because it is all different now, a new place, different slants and slashes and angles everywhere.

Salty slaps the ticket down on the counter as I take up my place behind it. "This is a ferry ticket," I say. "You need the pawn ticket."

Salty points at me and winks.

Is it like a game show? Is this what my dad's days were made up of? Is that what the big fat smile was about, because it was all one great goof all the time?

"Right," he says, and slaps down a new ticket.

"That's a receipt for fish and chips. Okay, right, just point out your thing. Where is it?"

The old man doesn't even need to look. He points at it about six feet up the wall, in the corner behind me, hanging there in a jumble of other old-timey noisemakers. There's a ukulele, bagpipes that look like a giant mounted spider, a shiny black clarinet.

I follow the pointing finger back there, step up on a little two-step, and bring my quarry down.

"What do you owe on it?"

Salty shrugs. "Dunno. Few bucks? A fiver?"

I am struggling. I'm struggling with my first-ever transaction of my new life. "Come on, guy," I say to the guy, "this can't be the way it works. I don't even want to take your money, but this thing"—I gesture with a broad sweep of my arm at all the *stuff*—"has to function somehow, and since you are clearly more experienced with it than I am, why don't you tell me what's supposed to happen here?"

"It'll be in the Testament," Salty says. He's pointing again, and I *get it*, that this place is more like the customer's than the proprietor's. There is a bank of drawers built right into the wall behind my station at the desk, and Salty is pointing down, at the bottom drawer.

I pull open the drawer, which fights me, and pull out a thick black leatherish three-ring binder. I throw it open to the middle and see lines after lines after lines of people's names and their accounts, their records, their phone numbers, their status, their *stuff*. Charlie Waters Sr. did not have normal-bad writing. He did not even have doctor-bad writing. He had head-injury-bad writing, but I could always read it, always took pride in that fact, and I'm enjoying it now more than ever, like it's some secret code the two of us are sharing across time and death and everything.

"Right," I say, "what's your name?"

"Seven."

I sigh. How could I be this fatigued, this early, on the first day of the welcome-to-the-world part of my life?

"That's a number, sir," I say.

"Right-o so. Let's try *Admiral Seven*."

I am sighing too much for a guy my age, but with another sigh, I flip to the A section of the binder, and there I find the listing for Admiral 7.

It's a substantial listing. Ol' number 7 has pawned, over the years, clothes, pots and pans, boxing gloves, wooden clogs, war medals, books, stuffed animals, scrimshaw, luggage, timepieces, motorcycle tires, baseball equipment, board games, pornographic magazines, exotic spices, original sheet music, unlisted phone numbers, a cat, coins, rocks, animal pelts, allegedly famous human teeth, house paint, gardening tools, life jackets, rare Pez dispensers, shrubs, lamps, flags, fossils, curtains, horseshoes, copper wire, more war medals but from a different war, a beer-making kit, and one item that just says "undying gratitude," for which he received six dollars.

There is a note, highlighted in yellow, that says the admiral may pay in installments, for the rare item he actually wants back.

The Testament says 7 owes five on his concertina.

"Says you owe five," says Charlie Waters's son.

Admiral 7 has a big broad smile and a full set of pearly teeth. The teeth are up on a shelf in the shop someplace, but the smile is right there in front of me as I hand over the little squeeze box.

"Had this sweet thing for forty years," Salty 7 says as he digs and digs around in his many pockets. He has sailor pants and that shorty sailor jacket, pockets inside, tiny breast pockets and hip pockets . . .

Which all together produce about a buck forty in coin. It is a long, sad sea change as Salty searches again the same dry pockets for the money that was probably there when he got off the boat yesterday but is long gone now. His puckered old face, too, shifts tides from high to low as the obvious finally comes obvious to him and he has to look at me all wrong.

How does it get to here? How does it get to where a guy like this with probably a million miles and stories and adventures and songs accumulated has to look embarrassed to a pale Lundy Lee whelp like me? Something went wrong, don't you think, for it to get here? Something got broken, didn't it?

I'm a broker now, funny enough. Pawn*broker* is my title, my legacy, my slot. Is it true? Is it accurate? Did my dad spend his hours breaking things? Breaking people? Is that who I am now?

"You must have dropped it somewhere," I say. "Happens, y'know?"

He turns his back to me, his face to the window,

to the distance, to the sea and the Big Island, where he has to go back concertina free.

He starts squeezing little squeezy noises from the concertina. Not a song assembly, not even what you might call notes. Squeelches. But little quiet ones.

"You like this jacket?" he asks, still with his back to me, still laying down eerie unpleasant background sounds.

It's not much of a jacket.

"It's a fine jacket."

"Gimme six for it?"

I'm thinking maybe, if it had seven in the pocket. Which, as we know, it doesn't.

"It's cold out, sir," I say. "You need that jacket."

"No, I *need* this concertina. Need it. Jacket has been all over the world," Salty says proudly.

One toilet at a time, from the smell of it. "I bet it has."

"Six, then?"

"Is that what the fat man would do?"

He spins and grins. Gives me a little shiver, actually.

"That's just what the fat man would do."

"I'd better do it then. A boy doesn't want to disappoint his dad, does he?"

Salty is already shedding the jacket as he heads my way. He slips it onto the counter and we shake hands, most of the money changing hands the way it always does in high finance, invisibly. I pull a fabricky tired dollar from my pocket and slide it across, and it looks very much like jackpot time for the salty seadog.

"You gonna play me something?" I ask. I don't know anything about the concertina, never heard one, never saw one, except in an old family photo of my uncle Otto, who legally married his while in prison. But it looks like something I would not like the sound of. But anyway . . .

The admiral throws his whole shrivel of self into the effort of squeezing that box and pressing those keys. It is a mighty effort, and a mighty sound that comes from it.

And even I know this is not what the thing is supposed to sound like.

Despite the joy on the old man's face, the impression is more of aggression. Like he has some kind of grudge with the concertina that has been building for all of those forty years and is going to be solved right here right now. Salty's efforts produce a squealing, bleating, screaming noise that all but pulls items down from shelves all over the shop. There is pain in this operation, and for the long three minutes it goes on, the instrument's reasonable response is just to cry.

Eventually it just stops, the way a car crash does, with an abrupt crunch. The old man looks at the young man, beaming. The young man looks back smiling, wincing, happy the old man is happy, happy it's over.

"That was an old Welsh sea shanty," the man says, "and at the end there, that was 'Greensleeves.'"

"I thought I heard that in there," I say as I step from behind the counter to see the man out before he attempts to encore. "That was lovely, sir."

My hand is on the man's back, gently suggesting to him the door, and the world outside it. The man is looking, or trying to look, behind him at the hand, like he's surprised, disbelieving, disappointed. The smell coming off the man, from up close, is rum and fish and a tiny spritz of urine. I breathe it in, a little put off, but then not as much as you might expect.

"You smell just like Lundy Lee," I say as I usher the man out to the sidewalk.

He nods, and his wind-worn happy face firms up serious. "Your dad was a fine man," Admiral 7 says, standing on the blank sidewalk with the ferry and the sea and the world off over his shoulder.

I take it. Start to answer, hitch back, look down at his feet briefly, then back up.

"So was yours," I say, even though I never met the old man's old man, even though he was probably dead already several wars ago. Because that's what Charlie Waters Jr. was taught by his dad. *Everybody's dad is a good man*, Charlie always told his boy. And why ever would I not believe him?

"Wanna go for a drink?" the admiral asks hopefully, fingering the keys on his deadly concertina.

"Thank you," I say, "but I have to run the show here."

I do not go back to running the show, however, until I have gone to the spot in the front window where the old man had been watching the sea. And I see that the sea was not really what he loved so dearly from this spot. I watch the salty old sea dog meander his way across the street, along the promenade, up to the establishments that want him as much as he wants them. He takes his unexpected $2.40 windfall and a squeeze-box full of good times and pours through the front door of the Compass Inn, right next door to the North Star Bar.

"I don't know, Dad," I say, still watching, still hearing the godawful misery of the concertina in my head. "Was that a good thing? On balance? Will the world forgive me for that? How do you know? How do you measure these things? What have you done to me here, Dad?"

I wait for an answer. I am somehow surprised when he does not provide me with one.

"You'll get back to me, then."

I head back to the job, and further into the life. I immerse myself in the Testament, working out who is who, matching up nicknames and details and figures with the hundreds of items lining the walls of Bread&Waters Loans.

And there is commentary, written in the margins of people's listings.

Too much jockey, not enough horse, it says in the

margin of a man who seemed to pawn a lot of women's dresses.

"What's that supposed to mean?" I say, laughing and tracing the path to the dress section. I am coming on fast now, into the business. I am learning right off to laugh at it all. And that you talk to yourself a lot in the pawn-broker business. "How is that supposed to help me, Dad . . . jockey, horse? Ya big fat fool."

I do a flinch. I'm not there yet, but I know only when I try. It's like jabbing myself with a knife still, saying that pointed wiseguy stuff. Dad is still my big fat hero. Crap-talking like he's here only calls attention to the big fat absence, which calls attention to the big fat gatekeeper no longer standing guard between Charlie Waters Jr. and "that rat-ass world" Dad always laughed about.

Six weeks before my father died, I bought him a big fat festive Hawaiian shirt. Because it was festive, it helped us both. How could bad things be coming to a man in a brand-new big fat festive Hawaiian shirt? They couldn't.

That's why I could go it even further. That's why— seeing big fat don't-you-goddamn-do-that eyes on my dad at receiving the shirt, the gift, the scaredy, and the message—that's why I could say to him, "Hey, old man, keep those tags on there, just wear them tucked inside, because I want to return the shirt after you're meat."

Because it couldn't possibly happen if you said stuff like that, could it? No, and then the great, massive pagoda-guy in the birds-of-paradise tent shirt could continue standing guard at the gate like always, like should-be.

I still have the shirt and the shirt still has the tags. In the closet in the house where the mail keeps coming anyway.

Back to the Testament. *Severe Gail, bordering psychotic*, it says, echoing the shipping forecast, next to the name of a woman who left a baby carriage three weeks ago and hasn't been back.

Dad loved that shipping forecast.

I loved Gail.

Gail McGill—I knew it right away. She was always a little bit nuts, all the way back to fourth grade, when she demonstrated her unlimited devotion to me by licking pigeon droppings off a picnic table. Devotion and insanity may have been indistinguishable in the nine-year-old mind, but Gail and I got along better than fine for a lot of years, until we went our separate ways. *Separate* meant the Y in the road that splits the main thoroughfare of Lundy Lee into two pointless directions inland. *Separate* meant I stayed on my old right fork while Gail traveled two miles and two babies up the other way, and while living in a place such as the Lee means everybody sort of knows everybody, it somehow means in a way that everybody eventually becomes a stranger too.

Gail pawned her baby buggy to my father.

I circle around from my place of authority to get over to the furniture section since, after all, what's a carriage but baby furniture with someplace to go. I find it, and find it to be one of the nicer items in the shop. It's one of those overspecial, overpadded all-terrain baby vehicles that, if they were a lot bigger and motorized, could work as a grown man's sleeping quarters *and* an eye-catching set of wheels to show off for the chicks. It has never been used. Or: It has been used by an uncommonly tidy and unbabylike baby, because this thing is showroom buff. And from the little bits of news that ever rolled down the two miles from Gail's world's end, her two babies (and very possibly an approaching third) were not even in the regular category of slop-slinging, tire-chewing, cat-scaring bundles of terror, never mind the extradelicate kind.

It's a buggy that made no sense. Maybe that's why she pawned it.

"Why are there so many Tuesdays?" I read out loud as I make my way back to my post. I read from the book like I'm reading from literature. I read to the assembled tools and toys and antique advertising signs like I'm reading to an audience of the willing.

You worsen the person, I read.

"How?" I ask. "How do you worsen them? And who is the person? You? Me? Them?"

Answer? None. Silence.

Alone again, but not alone enough, I sit frozen at the counter occupied for years by my father, the guv'nor, the beloved. Surrounded by the merchandise, the remains of the comings and the goings of the interactions of the relations of the customers/characters/clients/clandestines of Lundy Lee and the open sea.

The open sea. My body cannot move, but my eye is live. Out to the horizon. Out the big faded stenciled window, over parked cars, across the street, beyond the gapped grin of low salt-eaten buildings, to the sea, which is always in sight from just this spot where my father spent his progressively sedentary years. You can see a storm coming for miles from this spot, and I watch as one comes running right now. A charcoal avalanche of malevolent cloud is pushing its way across the chop face of the water so fast, it will be here in minutes. Wind begins to rattle the windows, and the first sharp dashes of rain begin hitting everywhere.

I love this. This, to me, is life. The universe giving Lundy Lee CPR, hammering its chest and blowing somebody else's air in to revive it if just for a little while, and it's a thrill.

It is almost a disappointment that I can see the end of the storm nearly as soon as I see the beginning. For seven, eight minutes, this thundering, blustering beauty pounds the front of the shop so hard that it could very well wind up letting itself in, but there, right behind it, comes the lightning-crack tail, following it home, passing overhead, whipsnapping, leaving the town wet and breathless and alone again gasping. I miss it already.

"Holy hell, huh?"

I barely look in the direction of the door as the kid ambles in. It's the lifeguard from the municipal pool, and he looks as if he has swum his way over in his clothes.

"Holy hell," I say with a wave.

"I timed that perfectly," the kid says. "Stepped out the door just as the thing blew in, then came in here just as it blew away again. Woulda stayed drier if I'd stayed in the pool."

"Isn't that where you should be?" I ask.

"Ah, not a problem. Nobody ever comes on Mondays. Ever. Just wind up talking to myself, and that ain't mentally healthy."

He is about two years older than me, but we have no history. He's just one of those people who wash up in this type of town, live above one of the shops for a while, doing this or that job nobody really needs them to do, then move on again. Nice enough guy, been here over a year already. You can hear the time ticking off of him.

"Wanna buy a ring?" the kid asks.

"Not really," I answer. Buying stuff had not really entered into my mind much. I knew, mostly, what the business was about, but until now I had not gotten my mind around the idea of bringing merchandise in. This was supposed to be my livelihood now, carrying on my dad's business, holding steady the core center of the "community" of Lundy Lee for the greater good and for life. But to be honest, I was thinking of it more in terms of outgo. Of seeing the current inventory delivered to the previous owners or the new owners, finishing up Senior's uncompleted business and then . . .

What? And then, what, Junior?

"Isn't that what you do?" Kid asks.

"I guess," I answer. I put out my hand.

Kid pulls a ring from his pocket, places it in my palm. The ring looks the real thing, a 1929 gold Indian head coin in a chunky ten-carat gold setting that looks like something a bishop would wear. The underside is open so you can see the details of the back of the coin, with a slick American eagle etched in it trusting in God and everything.

"I know next to nothing about jewelry," I say,

squinting at the ring and turning it over and over.

"Cool," Kid says. "Then it's worth two million."

"Sorry," I say, "but I left it in my other pants. Is it stolen?"

"No way. My mom gave it to my dad; then she ran away to find herself, before anybody ever knew she was lost."

"Did she find herself?"

"Not that I know of."

"Huh. Well my mother's looking too, so maybe if they don't find themselves they'll find each other."

"That would be very sweet. Anyway, then my dad and me went fishing, to forget her, like, and he threw the thing in the river near home. The only thing I can do great is swim, so when we went home and he went to sleep, that is just what I did, I swam. I went back to that lazy no-fish river and I dove in where we were, and didn't I find that gleaming shiny ring in about five minutes?"

"That's nice," I say. "But maybe, the way it happened and everything, it's like a sign or something that you should keep the ring."

"That's what I thought. But then I need money, like ya do, right? And I don't make dirt over there guarding nobody's life, watching nobody swim but me. So I came in here and I had to make a choice and I chose to keep the ring, but I put up a couple of trophies, my swimming trophies, for a few bucks with your dad. He was a fine guy too, your dad . . ."

"So is yours."

"Thanks. But I figured, like you figured, that I should have the ring. But know what? The ring doesn't make me happy. I been blue since the day my swimming trophies left me, and I think I made the wrong choice, y'know? So I was thinking, how 'bout you just give me those two trophies, I see them right there, the ones that have little divers on top that actually do look like me, and I will give you this ring and we will call it all square?"

I look over at the small swimming trophies. They aren't even nice trophies. Plastic. Chipping. One of them has the name plate glued on crooked.

"The ring's got to be worth about a thousand times as much as the trophies," I say.

Kid shakes his head, many times. He looks embarrassed, exposed, suddenly younger even than Junior. "Not really," he says, "not really, though. For one thing, your dad gave me too much to begin with. . . ."

"Why am I not surprised? I don't know how the man stayed afloat."

"And also . . . just, not really. Here, make the trade. Here, let's."

I still have the ring in my palm, bouncing it, weighing it up, when I retrieve the two little statuettes from the shelf. They weigh not much more than the ring.

Kid is reunited with the trophies, clutching both little divers with exactly that same grip Academy Award winners use when they get their mitts on the big one. Only he stares at them more like he has been reunited with long-lost loves—parents, siblings, children.

I suddenly feel something. I am overcome, overwhelmed, with a rush a of good feeling like I have not recognized before, certainly not in recent times, as I oversee the sad little reunion. I beam over the ceremony as if I have really accomplished something here instead of having done, really, nothing at all.

Can you see? Why a guy would want to do this? Why a complete, fully functional person would want to waste his hours and months doing this stupid business?

So this is what good really feels like.

So this is what Charlie felt like.

"I don't really need the ring," I say.

"But I really need the trophies," Kid says. "And I don't have money. Really I'm only part-time, part-part-time even, at the pool, so they don't pay me for but a few hours a week. Most of the time I'm just hanging around there for the swimming, and to have someplace to be, and so maybe a nice girl or something might come in."

I laugh as I force the ring back on Kid. "No, don't worry about it. You've been the highlight of my day, really. And I think I'm doing . . . what I should do."

Kid looks at his great bounty, then back at me with a suspicious, quizzical look. He takes one jokey, testing step toward the exit. "You gonna call a cop on me now or something? This some sick game?"

I wave my friendliest unthreatening good-bye.

Kid takes his luck while it's warm and continues on out. "Hey, I'm gonna do a swim, like a charity swim, from here out to the Big Island and back. For charity. You wanna sponsor me?"

"When's the swim?"

"Dunno. Maybe later today."

"What's the charity?"

I keep smiling and waving.

"Not sure. Something really sad, though."

I smile, I wave, I don't hold my breath. "Let me know."

It's visible, what my father meant. About this job maybe being a public service, about it maybe being central to the community. I could be getting ahead of myself, but right now it feels pretty all right what I'm doing. Could I be the guv'nor?

It must be ages I'm dreaming on that, because I hardly notice the door swing open. I hardly notice the rail-thin scarecrow of a man walking my way, walking through the door, top of his head bald as beefsteak, blond cornsilk fringe hanging down back and sides.

"What can I do for you?" I say, almost as a way to slow his coming at me.

He lopes his way over regardless, swinging far right

and left as he walks. He could fail a drug test from halfway across the room. His eyes are dewy and kind, smiling and unsettling.

"I am very, very, very sorry for your loss. For *our* loss," says the man. "My name is Beech, and I came to meet the new boss, hoping he's the same as the old boss. Right?" he says, smiling harder and shake-shocking my hand. "Like the Who song, right?"

"Right," I say. "I hope I'm mostly the same."

"*I* hope you are mostly the same," Beech says. "We *all* hope you are mostly the same. The *universe* hopes you are mostly the same."

I wait. The air goes still.

"I'll try," I say with a shrug I really put my back into.

More still air.

"Can I help you?" I ask after we have run out of polite.

"You can, my man. I am here to collect my rightful belongings."

"That's good." I nod energetically. "Rightful belongings are our business. Ticket?"

"No ticket," Beech says brightly.

I sigh. "Then how—?"

"It's in the safe," he says, pointing to the narrow closet door next to the stack of drawers right behind me.

"There's a safe?"

"That's what Charlie called it. I don't think it's a real safe, though. I think it's a closet."

It is a closet. Shelves along the left side, boxes and bags stacked floor to chin elsewise. There is a bare bulb hanging from an ancient cloth-wrapped cord, with a little chain attached, to illuminate all.

It illuminates very little, but it does cast enough buttery glow to leave me none the wiser. "What is it?" I ask.

"It's a Viking," he says, as if the question itself is puzzling.

"It's a Viking," I repeat, looking back over my shoulder at the customer.

He nods at me, friendly and understanding. "Don't be scared. It's not a real one, like from Denmark or something. It's a two-foot-tall statue of a hairy Viking leaning on a mace, and with one of those horny helmets and extra big feet. Did Vikings even use maces? I don't think that's really historically . . ."

I am already buried in the dim closet as Beech comes to his conclusion about the validity of the Viking's relationship to the mace. I dig, and things fall off shelves and something hard clomps me good right where the spine meets the head, but I find the historically dubious gentleman, swing him right around, and present him handsome on the counter.

They are clearly both happy to be reunited. Viking wears wide goose-egg eyes of excitement and a plunderer's grin through his beard. Beech wears practically the same expression.

There is an awkward moment. Like sitting on the bus next to some saddo whose birthday it is and somehow you just have to be made to know or he can't enjoy it.

"Check it out," Beech says slyly. "His head twists off like this. . . ."

The Viking is hardly headless before the whole room knows his secret. The grass crop tucked in his belly has a smell so strong, when the bag is opened I'm sure every dope-fiend seagull is going to crash into my front window within minutes.

"What have we got here?" I ask needlessly.

"My homegrown. Two exceedingly smooth ounces, if I may pat my own hairy back. Right, funny thing: I had this stuff, and then some other stuff, way different but interesting stuff in its own special way, y'know?" He is waving his hands and spindly fingers in the air between us as if he is trying to mesmerize us both. He's only batting .500 with the mesmerizing, but I am a little slack-jawed. "And this stuff doesn't come across these shores often, am I right?"

"I don't know if you're right," I say coldly. "Just finish the story."

"Okay, well I don't have a lot of time because this Afghanic guy is away on the next boat and I don't have enough bones to stand up a *cat*. But because of the reputation of your straight-up old man, and of Bread&Waters Loan Company as the only true-blue supporter of the local small businessmen of Lundy Lee—"

It's like the expression
world's oldest profession.

Everyone knows what everyone means
by *the local small businessmen of Lundy Lee*.

"That never happened," I say, as flat as the calm dead sea.

"Huh?" Beech asks, bumped right off his story.

"Your story isn't true. It did not happen, so you should just stop telling it now. My father did not know what is in that statue, because if he had, he wouldn't have kept it here."

Beech has visibly deflated. What was clearly one of his better days has now been run right into the ground.

And, bizarrely, I feel a pang of bad as I see him and his Viking lose their moment. I feel both totally, righteously right and guilty as hell, and it is one of the crappiest combinations ever and I cannot get them out of my shop fast enough.

Beech mutters something as he wrangles cash up out of a deep pocket and lays it out on the counter like a child with his coloring pages.

I point at the cash. "*That* is what he gave you, to pawn *him*?"

"Well, there's the what he gave me, and the what for interest, 'cause I'm late. I was in bed a few days with a fluish, and there's the what more, like usual, that I add on for the, y'know, profit thingy, which was better than usual because of the unusual opportunity that it was. He was the only guy," Beech adds wistfully, "ever support-ing the local small—"

"Just keep it," I say, gathering up the bills and tuck-ing them together the way careful people do with money. I hand them over. "We don't handle that kind of business here. Sorry."

Beech looks a little sad, a little lucky, but more sad, I believe. My heart likes that in its flickering way.

"In that case," Beech says, "you might want to give me that sacred heart statue up there on the top shelf. And leave his head on."

I think I hear myself laugh as I bring Jesus down from up there. Beech smiles and nods and backs away from the counter, clutching his twins. He turns and walks to the door with less of the side-to-side than he brought in, but turns in the doorway and calls back, "Your dad was a fine guy, no matter." He stands there firm with an I-mean-it look.

"So was yours," I say.

You can see that he can practically *smell* it when he backs into Lundy Lee's one honest-to-god cop. Clutching his treasure, Beech looks desperately back to me but doesn't give up the show.

I nod.

He goes.

He's not honest-to-god Lundy Lee's cop anyway, since Lundy Lee only rates a part-time presence from the district force. "Officer Fortnightly" is how the officer is prominently represented in the Testament.

"Good day, sir," I greet Officer Fortnightly.

"Good day to you, sir," Fortnightly responds, extending a warm and friendly hand of authority. "What was that numpty doing here?"

"Same as everyone, financing this glamorous lifestyle."

"Right," Fortnightly says, eyeballing the new proprietor to see if the relationship will be as shipshape as the old one was. "You are aware that the merchandise you take in is supposed to be registered with us, to prevent movement of stolen goods and contraband."

"Yes, sir."

"And you are supposed to get ID, and a picture. Nobody under eighteen?"

"Yes, sir."

The straightforward uncomplication of the conversation does not seem to agree with the lawman. In fact it seems somehow slightly to agitate him. He begins wandering around the shop, fingering items, picking them up and putting them down as if he is on a shopping trip, which he sort of is.

"I was sorry to hear—"

"He was a fine man, my dad, wasn't he?"

Officer Fortnightly is thrown for a second by the interruption. He stops his snooping, regards the boy businessman. "Yes," he says. "Your dad was a fine man."

"So was yours," I say brightly.

Fortnightly gets all forthrightly, marching right up to the counter, leaning right up to me. "You being wise with me?"

"I don't mean to be, sir."

"How old are you?"

"Nineteen."

"Really. You seem older."

"Should have seen me this morning before I opened up. I was a kid then."

We are inches from each other's faces. We stay there for a minute, trading breath. It is not a fair trade, as most trades aren't, and I begin to squint.

"I believe you have mail," I say, sliding an envelope across the desk. An envelope that was sealed and marked by the previous regime.

The door opens, and a girl comes in, a young woman. "Should I come back?" she says quickly.

"Please," I say, "do come in."

Officer Fortnightly takes his envelope and tucks it away. He gives me another smile and a stiffer handshake and wishes me the very, very best in my new life at the helm. "See you in two weeks," he says.

"Why?" I ask. Though I kind of know why.

Stumped, then not, he smiles. "To pick up my mail."

"Oh," I say. "That mail came from, like, the dead. Don't know if we'll be getting any more of that. You know how dead folks can be about keeping in touch. We'll let you know if any comes in."

He waves the envelope at me, waves my father's

beyond-embarrassing beyond-the-grave handwriting at me. "I'll see you in two," he says.

If I haven't retired by then.

"Hi, I'm Sandy," she says, and sandy she is. Hair, eyes, skin, all paled out like she's been oversoaked in seawater, hauled out, rung out, beaten on a flat rock, and left drying in the wind and sun for a while.

I'm in love with her already.

"Don't cops give you the creeps?" she says.

"Some of them," I say. "I'm Charlie."

"I know you," she says, pointing in a way that would be impolite if I did not know her. I don't know her, though.

"I know you," I say, hoping I do, pointing right back. "Why do I know you?"

"I met you in the hospital. I was working there . . ."

Whoosh. It comes hurtling in my direction, the vision of this girl, this young woman, this kind and heartbreaking psychiatric nurse being so kind to my mother the patient, and father, and me myself. The other thriving institution, at the other end of Lundy Lee, bookending the town with the ferry port. The mental hospital, short-term no-hope a specialty. My mother had a holiday there once.

"How is your mother?" she asks sincerely. She looks less healthy than she did when we last met. She looks smaller, and younger, and less like a nurse.

"I'm going to take a guess and say, 'Good,'" I say. "How are you?"

"I'm going to say . . . not so good. I don't work at the hospital now."

"No?"

"No."

Conversation grinds itself to a severe halt, after starting so promisingly.

"Um, can I help you with something?"

"Well," she says. "Yes. Yes. Yes, you can."

It is a conversation that does not seem to want to sustain itself.

"You have something you want to pick up? Something you want to buy, or sell?"

"Um," she says. "Um. Yes."

I wait. "Listen, you don't need to be bashful with me. You know, there's a lot of people coming in here with a lot of situations, so nothing is really too big a deal after a while, whatever—"

"We had . . . an arrangement."

I smile, happy to be getting somewhere.

"You had, what?"

It's like she's asking me now. "An arrangement? We had, kind of, a thing, me and your dad."

The adult section of my mind does a runner, off to the darkest recess where it won't be reached, while little-boy Charlie takes the controls.

"Right, lots of people did. That's the kind of business we have here, you know, arrangements between . . ."

It is too late, though, as the blood rushing to flush every part of my visible skin attests.

"But we had . . . an arrangement," she says softly, reaching out to pat my hand.

No. I loved, and love, every saturated fistful of fat that was my father. And my mother has been godknows-where doing godknowswhat with godknowswho for ages. But this youngish, prettyish lady climbing around over my father . . . in trade? For what? For a rabbit coat? A blender?

"A *what*?" I bark, withdrawing hand and self from her. "A *thing*? What's a *thing* . . . Sandy? With *my* dad? What's a thing? With my dad? No, I don't think you did."

"I think I did."

Betrayed simultaneously, instantaneously by a lovely dead fat man and the shiny new stranger love of my life, I am hunched with hurt and not intent on a healthy exchange of ideas with Sandy at the moment. I flip open the Testament and find her there, nearly hyperventilating as I read the word *arrangement* in the margin. I am too slow, though, to stem the flow, to get clear, as my eyes fall a few lines down to Steven, and the marginal *arrangement*. And on, and on, the word *arrangement* now written in boldface, leaping off the pages at me now from six different spots on this spread alone,

"I would just get my stuff back—without giving him any money—is all," Sandy says, uninvited. "It was okay. It was okay both ways. It was good."

"Could you leave, please? Could you leave? Sandy. Sandy Arrangement? Please?"

"I just thought that, considering, maybe you're lonely just like—"

"Maybe not. Could you leave, please?"

"I would guess this is a lonely job here—"

"Please," I snap, and stare at the counter, at the Testament.

Sandy's quick breath comes out in choppy little bursts like the surf. She bites her lip and quick steps to the door.

"I don't want you to think any bad thoughts about your father. He—"

"Don't bother telling me what a fine guy he was. Just don't bother."

She turns around snappish and shouts, "He *was*! He was a lovely fine man, way more than you could ever be!"

I actually leap over the counter after her, and smack right into the thick glass door as she slams it on me. I remain there, pressed to the glass, closing my eyes, letting my hot cheek cool with the contact.

I walk so slowly back to the counter, I feel like a flower wilting in real time. I walk straight to the safe, the closet, the stash. I begin pulling things down and find guns. I find jewelry that for some reason cannot play with the jewelry out in the display case. I find photographs, men with women, men with men, taken from far away. I find loose gold teeth. I find bottles and bottles of pills. I find a finger in a box, dried like a long stick of dehydrated mango.

This is what it means to be the guv'nor.

In the door walks Andy LeBue, the world's most godawful comic. He worked the local VFW until every last vet died of ill humor and the place closed down. Then he bounced between the ferry and the bars, working for coins until people stopped paying him to perform, then stopped paying him to shut up. He wears a rug on his head that was made for a head much smaller, and carries a blue-haired ventriloquist's dummy named Blue that looks less scary than most because he looks so embarrassed.

"How are you supposed to tell which one's the village idiot in a village like this?" Andy asks Blue, or Blue asks Andy, who can tell?

"I have a gun back here, Andy," I say.

"Ah"—Andy laughs—"you know how often I hear that? How much will you give me for Blue, here?"

"I don't wanna stay here," Blue protests.

"He's a nice boy," Andy says soothingly. "I knew his dad. His dad always laughed for us. I loved his dad."

And, for this.

For this, after all. For this, Charlie Waters Jr. begins to well up with an ocean's salty tears. I keep them in the well, though.

"As a public service, for the sake of everybody in town, I'll give you thirty for Blue, and I'll give him a loving home until you come back."

"See?" Andy says, both visibly happy and broken as he hands Blue over. "I told you he was his father's boy. Now I don't want to say Charlie Waters was fat, but I once saw him open a door with a burp."

Andy looks shocked when I start to laugh. Something in there, in that stupid joke, felt so good and honest and real about the old man that it gave me an immense release of something better, spreading through my belly, lungs, and ribs.

Andy is fairly fleeing as Blue and I stand there, both

waving him good-bye. "See you soon," says Blue.

It is only lunchtime.

"Jesus H. Jesus," I say, slumping exhausted into the low upholstered chair with the gigantic ass crater that sits behind the counter. It is positioned so that, no matter what, if you just had to collapse back there, you almost had no choice but to land in the chair. The chair sort of stinks. But it certainly is comfortable.

Blue is on my lap, and the Testament is in my hand. I flip it open with a great deal of trepidation. I open to the very first page, which I had not seen earlier. Come what may, Charlie Waters Jr. is going to read this book cover to cover, line for line, and every line in between.

It begins with a sort of title page. *PRIVATE*, it says in that mentalist handwriting scratch.

FOR THE EYES OF CHARLIE WATERS ONLY

I smile at the joke I share with my dad. How fantastically pointless that the only two people in the world who could read that warning were both named Charlie Waters.

Page two is blank; page three is a kind of dedication page, an inscription, as if this would be a real book.

JUDGMENT DAY WAS YESTERDAY.
SORRY, NO REFUNDS.

This is his book. This is Charlie's Testament. And Charlie's boy is reading it, come what may.

But it is lunchtime. So it may come after lunch. Dad would agree.

I flip to S. I dial her number.

She is still chopping that sad quick breathing like the surf as she answers the phone.

"This *is* a lonely job," I tell her. "You want to do good for people, but what's good? You want to be a fine guy, but what's fine? You want to try, but trying is hard and it's exhausting and, hell, it's only lunchtime on day one.

"But I could buy lunch, Sandy," I say to her, hopefully. "I could do that much, I know. Buy us lunch at the Compass or the North Star, watching the water?"

Dave Chester, 2007

Chris Lynch is the author of the National Book Award finalist *Inexcusable* as well as many highly acclaimed books for young adults, including *Me, Dead Dad, & Alcatraz,* the Michael L. Printz Honor Book *Freewill,* and *Iceman, Shadow Boxer, Gold Dust,* and *Slot Machine,* all four ALA Best Books for Young Adults and winners of several other prestigious awards, and *The Big Game of Everything* and *Cyberia.* He holds an MA from the writing program at Emerson College and lives in Scotland with his family.

The Company

Jacqueline Woodson

The damn ankle is sprained. It won't do the right thing. Twisting and buckling. Me trying to be fabulous across the stage and landing on my ass. The ankle's some new stranger, swollen and weak. So now they're calling this my *sabbatical*. The head of The Company—I'm gonna call him Roger to protect myself if he decides he wants to try to sue or kick me out of The Company or holler—Roger says just stay off it awhile. Ice it. Put it up. Rest and shit. Like it's that damn easy to sit my ass down and not dance. He is such a *queen*. You didn't hear it from me. Oh no you didn't. Just this morning I'm sitting up in here with the ankle reading the *New York Post* and there he is—getting some award and showing all those teeth. The article's got the nerve to go on about him being single and having no kids but hoping

to one day have a family of his own. "But for now," the article blah-blah-blahed, "he's got his Company." That shit burns me up. How is someone gonna look right at Roger and not see *queen*? Snow queen at that—almost six foot four, blue-black and beautiful, walks up in the studio most mornings with that white man trailing behind him all quiet and handling things. Well, that's what they got him on the books doing. *Accounting.* I know what he's accounting. He's accounting Roger—rocking him like a boat up in that grand old Harlem brownstone they got going on. And both of them way past thirty trying to rock it like us young people, partying and whatnot. Some days, I'm hoping I never get that old and have to watch all the beautiful children moving by me all free and easy and ready for whatever's coming. Those two queens look more like they're ready for rocking chairs. Even if Roger can still move through the air like one of us, you can see the living he's done all up in his face and around his eyes and in the way he looks so damn *tired* at the end of the day.

A few months after I joined The Company, Roger had himself a little soirée, as he called it—supposed to be straight and talking about a *soirée*. When was the last time anybody heard a straight man call a party a *soirée*? So of course I went—me and Tony kee-keeing our way on the train all the way from Brooklyn—that's where I was living then—to that pretty brownstone where Roger and—surprise, surprise—Snow were having their soirée. When me and Tony got there, Roger introduced us to Snow (I'm not even bothering to come up with a better name for him. Snow's real name is one that's so different that if I said it, everyone would know who I was talking about, and as I said, I'm not trying to get myself thrown from The Company.) Snow's darker than real snow but not much. His eyes are blue like you see on the white men in movies—those white men Tony gets stupid over but I can't see any beauty in. Tony claims he ain't a snow queen in the making but . . . *well*. Give me tall, dark, and handsome. And when I say dark, I don't mean tan either. And I don't mean Roger, because me and him on the same side of this here queen fence and nothing either one of us can do for the other. People can talk all that junk about being *fluid* and *not ascribing* to roles and calling it *that back-in-the-day crap* and whatever whatever, but I don't see anything wrong with a person knowing who and what they like. I like them dark and ready to make their mark. I like them long and strong. If I wanted a somebody who hee-heed with his hand covering his mouth, and put one pinky in the air to drink his damn tea, well I could just laugh and drink tea and look in the mirror—could just date my own damn self.

The first time I learned Tony liked himself some snow, we were getting ourselves together after dancing all day long. It must have been October because I remember us both having a lot of stuff with us—in the summer, you see dancers with their bags all light and whatnot, but fall and winter it is all about the layers. Sweat all day and be freezing if it's anything below eighty outside. Me and Tony'd met the month before, when both of us got signed to The Company. I was seventeen and Tony was nineteen, and he already had himself a place. I was still living with my mom, and since I was going to get paid sweet for being in The Company, I was telling him about it being time for me to bounce from her space.

I'm looking for a roommate, Tony said. We'd already changed out of our dance clothes into sweats and boots, had already thrown our jazz shoes, leg warmers, and dance clothes in our bags. I'd danced hard that day—being fabulous, my kicks higher than I'd ever seen the legs go and my arms all up and over the place but *controlled*, because Roger's first words to me had been that I need to rein my dancing in—that I was talented but needed to learn control. His exact words? *"Let's leave the street in the street"*—and even though I'd wanted to snap and let him know nothing about me was street, I just kept my mouth closed because he was Mr. Charlie now. The Boss Man. He was Money in My Pocket and Holder of My Dream. So I'd kept *control* and danced hard. So hard, I could smell my funky, sweaty dance clothes right through the canvas bag my mama had given me as both a high school graduation and a congrats on making The Company present.

I gave Tony a look. Tony's biracial—which means two things—not my type and pretty in that curly-hair, red-skin sort of way. Some of the girls in The Company were already giving him the look, because straight girls don't be caring sometimes—you can be gay as you want to be and they'll still come knocking for a knocking. What is that *about*? And some of the guys dipped into the fish tank every now and then, but I wasn't one of them and one look at Tony and I knew he'd been gay since he took his first baby steps across the room. I knew his daddy probably said, "What's wrong with that boy? Why is he walking like that?"

So when he asked about a roommate, I knew right away I'd have to let him know me and him wasn't going to happen.

"A roommate, huh?" I said.

"Yeah, a roommate." Tony said. He threw his bag over his shoulder. "Rent's cheap, but I'm not trying to swing it on my own."

"How've you been swinging it?" I was wearing Timberlands and was busy trying to get the laces right. I had a long train ride home, and it's good to look as butch as you can on the subway so brothers don't start talking that mess they like to talk. And so those old men who are on their way home to their tired wives and whiny children don't start rubbing themselves on the sly while eyeing you.

"I had a friend living with me. But he moved out."

"A friend, huh? Now you trying to get me to be your 'new friend'?"

Tony looked at me a minute. Then he threw his head back and laughed. I hadn't seen him laugh before, and I liked it. The way it just came out of nowhere like that. Real honest, you know?

"Man I am *SO* not trying to push up on you," Tony said. "I mean, you're cute and all, but that's not how I roll."

It wasn't until after I moved in that I learned Tony rolled snow. I guess if you half snow yourself, you can see the beauty in it.

So that's how we ended up living together. The place was sweet—two bedrooms, with a kitchen and a living room between them. Lots of light, and Tony being a big plant guy, he'd already put lots of plants all around— in the bathroom and kitchen and on the living-room windowsill. The apartment looked out over a small park, and sometimes I'd look out my window and see the little kids swinging and running and climbing and it made me think I want something like that—a family. Some kids. Maybe even a big old black dog. And it made me wonder if I'd ever have it. And if I *was* going to have it, it made me wonder with who. I didn't want to be one of those fake-ass straight guys tryna have a *normal* life, kicking it with their wives while they think about guys like me. That was crazy. I wanted my old queenie self and somebody to love me for being the girl-boy I am. Wasn't deep.

When I was five, my daddy left. Not regular—like, *Here's a big fight with me and my woman and now I'm packing some stuff and getting the hell out.* Seemed a lot of the people I knew whose daddies left either had some kind of jump-off somewhere and finally just moved in with them or the parents just fought all the time until the daddy finally said, "I'm done. I'm gonna get my own place." And then for a while he's trying to stay in touch with the kids and all—taking them out for ice cream on a Saturday afternoon or taking them to the park and sitting on a bench while they pushed their own damn selves on the swings and whatnot.

My daddy left different. Summer, he'd always take us to White Castle—the burger joint that was kinda far from where we lived. After church, we'd all walk back to the house—me, him, my sister, Marie, and my moms. We'd be dressed up in our churchgoing gear—me always in some damn ugly tie because my daddy wore a tie and he thought every man needed a tie. And even though I was only eight, he was steady trying to man me up, and so Sunday came, he was standing behind me in the mirror showing me how to tie that damn thing. Always felt like a noose, and some mornings I'd get to pulling on it, having these deep visions of people swinging from trees somewhere. I didn't know then that it was my daddy trying to choke the faggot out of me. "Tie it like this, son," he'd say. My daddy was tall and beautiful—deep brown skin, a thick head of nappy hair, and shoulders like a plank across his chest. I'd stand in front of him looking at the two of us in that mirror—me all skinny and standing with my hip stuck out until he snapped at me to stand up like a man, and him all broad and handsome and strong behind me—all the things I'd never be. I'd stand there feeling the weight of that tie and his able hands flying through the air making that perfect knot, then untying it again and saying, "Your turn, brother man." And then my hands all clumsy doing it all wrong, never understanding how one end moved into the other, how one loop knotted into something straight and even and sure like that. And standing there sometimes, watching my daddy trying to help me figure it out, it was all I could do not to start crying like a baby because a big-ass part of me knew I wasn't ever gonna be the man my daddy wanted his baby boy to grow into.

Yeah—my daddy left different. Every Sunday, we walked the six blocks home from church, our perfect churchgoing family—Mama, Daddy, me, and Marie. Then me and Marie would change out of our church clothes and Daddy would take us on two buses to the White Castle over in Brownsville. Mama'd stay at home, lie down on the couch, and catch up on her Bible studies.

I guess from the outside it might look all stereotypical and whatnot. Bible-thumping Mama and deadbeat dad. That ain't where I'm going, though. Mama read that Bible because she liked good stories. She wasn't trying to convert nobody or get her preaching on. Sometimes she'd get so into Noah bringing those two-by-two animals or Lot's wife looking back and turning to a pillar of salt that she'd take out a notebook and start writing her own stories. She said the Bible inspired her, but not to be no God-fearing sister. Just to write. And mostly, my Mama just wanted to write.

The day my daddy left, it was raining. We didn't have umbrellas, but me and Marie had our raincoats and rain hats and we probably looked real corny, but I tell you, my rain set was red and it was fierce, and when I put it on, you couldn't tell me nothing about nothing. Marie's was yellow, all traditional like her. She was two years older than me and had two long braids and I swear it took her a long-ass time to work those braids up under her rain hat before we left the house. Mama had straightened her hair the night before, and she didn't want the rain making it all curly again, so she tucked and tucked, and by the time we left the house all rain-geared up, you couldn't see one strand of my sister's hair.

I wish I could remember what we ate at White Castle. I wish I could remember what we talked about. I wish I could remember if I saw something in my daddy's eyes that afternoon that gave me some clue that that was going to be the last day of tie tying and churchgoing and White Castling with him.

"I'll be right back," my daddy said. He glanced at Marie and said, "You keep an eye on him."

Me and Marie sat in that White Castle all afternoon. The rain stopped coming down. People came in, bought bags of burgers and left. Cars pulled up and ordered from the drive-through window, the voices of the people inside sounding all loud and gravelly. Marie had eaten three burgers and had two left. I had one left. By the time we reached in the bag to eat the rest of our food, it was near dark outside. I don't remember either one of us saying anything for most of the afternoon.

But then Marie got up, threw out all our trash, and said, "You wait here." And that's when I started crying like a baby. Then Marie started crying and the teenager who'd just been selling burgers and fries and looking at us every now and then picked up the phone behind the counter.

That's when the cops came.

✱

The night of Roger's soirée, me and Tony got dressed real nice—he wore this blue shirt that was shimmery—said he'd got it at H&M for cheap, but it looked like something that cost more than a shirt you'd get at H&M. I didn't know then that it was actually from Armani, but I'll get to that in a bit. And he had on some jeans that fit him real cool. I was looking fabulous myself—red turtleneck fitting me all tight and some black pants. It was December, and New York had gotten crazy already with the decorations—lights on every avenue. Christmas music coming from everywhere. Whole buildings blinking red and green and gold. Lit-up candy canes on lampposts. Me and Tony lived in Fort Greene—in Brooklyn, right off of Fulton Street—and as we walked, we looked inside different restaurants and kept seeing all those damn straight couples that come out to be in holiday love around that time of year. We walked to the subway talking about this and that, making fun of the couples and planning what we'd drink first when we got to Roger's—I was gonna throw back a rum and Coke and Tony said he was gonna start slow, with some white wine. Mostly we talked about dancing, though. I'd wanted to be a dancer since I could crawl.

"How'd you know?" Tony asked as we stood there waiting for the train that would take us straight up to Harlem.

I looked at him.

"You really want to know?"

"Wouldn't be asking if I didn't."

"I was watching *Zoe's Dance Moves*—that Muppets video with Paula Abdul in it."

Tony laughed that crazy big laugh. "Man, I used to *love* that!"

"Me too. My moms said she'd try to turn off the TV and I'd just start hollering."

"So that's when you knew?"

I shook my head. "That's when my *moms* knew. She said when I was nine months old, I stood up all wobbly and whatnot. And then I put one hand on the couch to balance myself and just started moving. She said I walked across that floor like I'd been walking for a year instead of two minutes."

"You lying."

"Nah, I ain't. Swear to God. Two days later, I'm standing in the center of the living room . . ." I did a spin and one of the kicks from the video. "And I'm doing the whole routine."

"For real?"

"For real as I want to be. How about you?"

Tony walked to the edge of the platform, then leaned over and looked for the train. Nothing was coming.

"I just danced all the time," he said. "And my dad said to butch up and act like a man."

His voice got real quiet.

"He said, '*You keep dancing like that, you're going to grow up to be a faggot.*'" Tony looked at me. "And since I knew I already was a faggot, I kept on dancing." He circled his arms, did a perfect brisé, and landed in arabesque. Tony moved like he'd always been moving.

"You are too fabulous," I said. "And I know your ass ain't get that shirt from H&M."

Tony smiled but didn't say anything. He was wearing a dark wool coat over the shirt. The coat reminded me of my mother. A week after my daddy left, she put her writing notebooks up into the closet, and me and Marie never saw them again. Two weeks later, she took a job cleaning people's houses, and sometimes they gave her their old clothes. A year after my daddy left, she came home with a brown coat like Tony's. I always hated the clothes she brought home, but something about that coat took the hatred to a whole new level.

"That coat's from Bloomingdale's," my mama said. "You're gonna put it on and wear it till it's so raggedy it falls off your skinny behind."

Mama held the coat out to me and I just stared at her—all the hate in my body seeping past that coat right on up to her.

"I ain't wearing no white people's old clothes anymore," I said.

Sometimes you wish you could just chassé your ass way back in time and snatch all the nasty stuff you did and said and thought back out of the world. It's like it hangs there, in the air, forever. And every time you look back into the past, it's there, screaming back at you— your own dumb-ass words, all loud inside your head again.

Mama looked at me, closed her eyes for a moment, then left the room. I never saw the coat again.

"Where'd you get that coat?" I asked Tony.

He shrugged, then checked the track again. I could hear a train.

"It's coming," Tony said.

Class shit is funny. Either you got crazy dollars and you don't want anybody to know, or you grew up broke and don't want anybody to know. Either way, for a little while, you meet in the middle—like me and Tony had done—trying to just gray out that shit and be.

The train was crowded. Me and Tony stood by the door, Tony with his foot bent up on it, looking around. At Borough Hall a couple of people got off, and me and Tony sat down across from each other, him with his legs all spread and butch until an old black lady got on at Park Place and gave him a look that made him close them up so she could squeeze into the little bit of space between him and a heavyset lady. Some punk-asses stood against another train door giving me fever. I paid them no mind and could hear them laughing. One said, "How *you* doing?" all sissylike to his friend. Yeah, I had a *how-you-doing* for him, but I wasn't about to get up and read his baby-punk ass unless he tried talking some junk directly to me. Me and Tony looked at each other but didn't try to sit there talking across the subway car. Tony leaned back and squeezed himself in. The old lady gave him a look and moved over one whole inch.

Last year Marie called me. She was finally finishing up her graduate stuff and had been offered a job in California, where she'd been going to school. We talked about this and that and how she was hoping to get to New York by Christmas to see me in my first solo and whatnot. Both of us knew it wasn't going to happen. After my daddy left, it was like Marie left too. She made Mama transfer her to a school on the other side of Brooklyn and started taking the train by herself everywhere. Then she got into a high school in Manhattan that was for strange smart-ass kids like she'd turned out to be. After that, seems we saw less and less of her until she was going to college. You'd think that something like what my daddy did would have made us mad close and scared of losing any more of our family. But it kind of had the opposite effect. We all just sort of went to our own little corners to figure out our own little lives. But that morning when the phone rang, Marie sounded real different. There was a lot of quiet in the conversation, like there was something she wanted to say but couldn't. Then she finally came out and said it.

"I saw Daddy last week," she said.

I felt something inside me drop away. It'd been ten years since I'd seen my father, and some parts of me had forgotten about him. But most of me hadn't.

"Yeah?" I said. I felt like I was nine years old again and wanted to ask her if he'd asked about me, if she'd told him I made The Company, if he regrets that Sunday—so many questions all crazy up inside my head.

"He's doing well," Marie said. "You know, we have a brother and a sister in Chicago."

"Nah," I said. "I didn't know that."

"Yeah," Marie said. "He moved there after he left . . . New York."

"How'd you see him?"

Marie didn't say anything for a while. Then she said, "I went looking. I called around. Did a little research, talked to some people, and finally tracked him down."

I was in my and Tony's apartment, standing by the window. Outside, the sun was bright white and cars were moving slow back and forth along the street. I couldn't hear anything but Marie's voice in my ear.

"He ask about me?" I finally said. Even as I said it, I was hating on myself for even wanting to know.

"You know he did. He's real proud."

"Yeah," I said. We talked for a little while longer. Marie said if I wanted, she'd send me all his info. I told her I'd let her know.

Me and my sister haven't really spoken since then.

A few days later I moved out of Tony's place and found my own up near where Roger and Snow live. It's small, has some good light coming in; and there's a few other queens up in the neighborhood, so I don't be having a lot of problems. Yesterday, this cool homeboy saw me limping with this damn ankle and my laundry and offered to carry it up the stairs for me. I let him, and even though he reads mad butch, turns out he's one of the children. Come Saturday, we heading over to Ruthie's Fish Fry for dinner, then checking out a movie.

The night Tony and me went to Roger's soirée, the whole company got to really hang for the first time. We drank and smoked and gossiped about Roger and Snow, then showed our stuff when Roger finally put on some music worth moving to. Roger was in rare form—pouring drinks and proudly bragging about us like we were *truly* his children. When he got to Tony, he was halfway drunk and said, "Don't ever tell me rich boys can't dance," and Tony smiled, but it was the saddest smile I'd ever seen on a person.

A week after the party, there was Tony in the Sunday Styles section of the *The New York Times*—pictured with his mama, who, it turns out, surprise, surprise, lives on the Upper East Side and comes from a long-ass line of rich people.

"Is this your people, Mr. H&M?" I asked Tony that Sunday morning. We were sitting at the kitchen table—him drinking coffee, me drinking a glass of orange juice and eating a leftover egg sandwich.

Tony shrugged and said, "Yeah."

We didn't say anything for a moment. It was like the line that divided us had gotten a whole lot thicker.

"We still cool," Tony said. "Right?"

"Yeah," I lied. "We cool."

The damn ankle swells when I put too much weight on it. But the damn legs hurt from not dancing, and the whole body feels like it's trying to jump out of itself to *move*.

The Company's performing *Giselle* at the end of

the month. Tony has the part of Count Albrecht. I'll be there. I'll cheer him on from third row center. Roger says it's not "The Company." It's "The Family." And I guess, this being the world I'm living in now, it's high time I get to realizing that, yeah, it's true—we're a big-ass, complicated, all shadows-and-secrets-and-hopes-for-a-different-future kinda family.

Marty Umans

Jacqueline Woodson was awarded Newbery Honors for her books *Feathers* and *Show Way*, and was a National Book Award finalist for her books *Hush* and *Locomotion*, the latter of which also received a Coretta Scott King Honor, as did her books *I Hadn't Meant to Tell You This* and *From the Notebooks of Melanin Sun*. *Miracle's Boys* won the Coretta Scott King Award and the *Los Angeles Times* Book Prize. Woodson won the Margaret A. Edwards Award for lifetime achievement in writing for young adults and, most recently, the Virginia Hamilton Literary Award. Woodson lives with her partner and family in Brooklyn, New York. You can visit her online at www.jacquelinewoodson.com.